He'd never realized and desire were linked....

Joe knew the exact moment that Penny came through the doors of the police station. He couldn't see her yet, but he heard the buzz, felt a slight shift in atmosphere, as though everyone had come to attention.

Because she intrigued him—and because she was so closemouthed about her life these past years—he'd done a simple background check on her. He hadn't intended to. A few taps on the computer keys and he'd found himself typing in Penny's name.

He'd been stunned to find no trace of her. It was as though she didn't exist—had *never* existed.

Whatever work she actually did had to be highly classified, and most likely dangerous, if someone had gone to the trouble to remove her identity from every computer data bank he'd known to access.

At that moment, she turned and met his gaze.

His heart actually thumped behind his breastbone. A pure shot of adrenaline turned his knees to jelly—much the same feeling as facing the business end of a gun in a dark alley....

Dear Reader,

Happy New Year! May this year bring you happiness, good health and all that you wish for. And at Harlequin American Romance, we're hoping to provide you with a year full of heartwarming books that you won't be able to resist.

Leading the month is *The Secretary Gets Her Man* by Mindy Neff, Harlequin American Romance's spin-off to Harlequin Intrigue's TEXAS CONFIDENTIAL continuity series. This exciting story focuses on the covert operation's much-mentioned wallflower secretary, Penny Archer.

Muriel Jensen's *Father Formula* continues her successful WHO'S THE DADDY? series about three identical sisters who cause three handsome bachelors no end of trouble when they discover one woman is about to become a mother. Next, after opening an heirloom hope chest, a bride-to-be suddenly cancels her wedding and starts having intimate dreams about a handsome stranger, in *Have Gown, Need Groom*. This is the first book of Rita Herron's new miniseries THE HARTWELL HOPE CHESTS. And Debbi Rawlins tells the emotional story of a reclusive rancher who opens his home—and his heart— to a lovely single mother, in *Loving a Lonesome Cowboy*.

In February, look for another installment in the RETURN TO TYLER series with *Prescription for Seduction* by Darlene Scalera.

Wishing you happy reading,

Melissa Jeglinski
Associate Senior Editor
Harlequin American Romance

THE SECRETARY GETS HER MAN

Mindy Neff

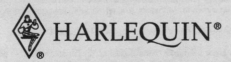

TORONTO • NEW YORK • LONDON
AMSTERDAM • PARIS • SYDNEY • HAMBURG
STOCKHOLM • ATHENS • TOKYO • MILAN • MADRID
PRAGUE • WARSAW • BUDAPEST • AUCKLAND

Special thanks and acknowledgment are given to
Mindy Neff for her contribution
to the Texas Confidential series.

This book is for Nancy Dayton and Jim Jones—
river neighbors, and friends. You guys are the greatest.

ISBN 0-373-16857-8

THE SECRETARY GETS HER MAN

Copyright © 2001 by Harlequin Books S.A.

Visit us at www.eHarlequin.com

Printed in U.S.A.

ABOUT THE AUTHOR

Originally from Louisiana, Mindy Neff settled in Southern California, where she married a really romantic guy and raised five great kids. Family, friends, writing and reading are her passions. When not writing, Mindy's ideal getaway is a good book, hot sunshine and a chair at the river's edge with water lapping at her toes.

Mindy loves to hear from readers and can be reached at P.O. Box 2704-262, Huntington Beach, CA 92647.

Books by Mindy Neff

HARLEQUIN AMERICAN ROMANCE
644—A FAMILY MAN
663—ADAM'S KISS
679—THE BAD BOY NEXT DOOR
711—THEY'RE THE ONE!*
739—A BACHELOR FOR THE BRIDE
759—THE COWBOY IS A DADDY
769—SUDDENLY A DADDY
795—THE VIRGIN & HER BODYGUARD*
800—THE PLAYBOY & THE MOMMY*
809—A PREGNANCY AND A PROPOSAL
830—THE RANCHER'S MAIL-ORDER BRIDE†
834—THE PLAYBOY'S OWN MISS PRIM†
838—THE HORSEMAN'S CONVENIENT WIFE†
857—THE SECRETARY GETS HER MAN

*Tall, Dark & Irresistible
†Bachelors of Shotgun Ridge

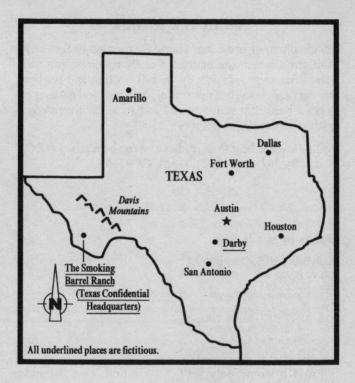

Amarillo

Dallas

Fort Worth

TEXAS

*Davis
Mountains*

Austin
★

Houston

Darby

The Smoking
Barrel Ranch
(Texas Confidential
Headquarters)

N

San Antonio

All underlined places are fictitious.

Chapter One

Penny Archer stepped a little harder on the throttle of her sleek black Cadillac as the headlights caught the reflective road sign announcing Darby, Texas five miles ahead.

Along the gravel shoulder of the road, a deer paused, eyes shining bright in the flash of headlights. Penny eased up on the gas. She'd been traveling for close to six hours and it wouldn't do to play a game of chicken with the wildlife. From past experience, she knew the Caddie would end up on the losing end of the deal if it came down to a collision.

And it would only set her back time-wise. In and out, she promised herself. She'd get her grandmother's affairs in order, sell the house, touch base with a couple of her high school friends, then get the heck out of Dodge—or Darby, rather.

She wondered if she'd subconsciously chosen the cover of darkness to return to her hometown that she'd only visited twice in the past twelve years.

Memories rolled over her—some painful, some embarrassing and some that were gentle, warm and irreplaceable.

She felt bad that she hadn't been here for her grandmother's funeral. Agnes Archer had been a pistol of a woman, tough to get along with, bitter, but nobody deserved to die and be buried alone. If it hadn't been for the latest case the Texas Confidential unit had been working on, Penny would have come. But she'd been tied up and the funeral had taken place without her.

Uncharacteristically, Penny flipped down the visor and checked her appearance in the lighted mirror as she turned onto Main Street. The image staring back at her gave her a momentary jolt. An hour back, when she'd stopped for gas, she'd impulsively exchanged her stylish, wire-rimmed glasses for a pair of contact lenses. Vanity wasn't normally part of her makeup, but some devil had urged Penny to take off the glasses, to play up her assets, to show off the good bone structure she'd enhanced with a few cosmetics.

Annoyed with herself, she flipped the visor back in place. It was as dark as sin out, for heaven's sake. The sidewalks in town had been rolled up by five no doubt and it was after eleven now. Not another soul was on the road. Who did she expect to see? Or impress?

An image of a boy with dark hair, broad shoulders and gentle brown eyes flashed like a strobe in her brain and she immediately cut it off. Her life was on a different course now and there wasn't room for foolish fantasies.

For the past twelve years, Penny had been working as Mitchell Forbes's executive assistant in the highly secretive Texas Confidential organization. She knew the cases and the agents better than anyone. And although her position with Texas Confidential was important and fulfilling, lately Penny had yearned for more. She hadn't quite been able to put her finger on what that ''more'' was until she'd single-handedly apprehended a band of cattle rustlers who'd been plaguing the Smoking Barrel ranch—Texas Confidential headquarters—for months. The adrenaline rush, the sense of accomplishment and the recognition and praise she'd gotten from her friends and colleagues had given her the courage to tell Mitchell that she wanted a more active role in the agency.

She wanted to be an agent.

Mitchell had agreed, and by this time next month, she would begin her training. But first she had to take care of her grandmother's estate.

And perhaps, to a certain degree, Penny needed to face up to her past before she could actually move on. Where that thought came from, she had no idea. And it made her more than a little uncomfortable.

Through the Cadillac's heavily tinted windows, she gazed out at the dark storefronts where shadowy mannequins posing in the boutiques seemed to follow the progress of her car as she passed. The crazy thought had Penny laughing out loud. She'd obviously been hanging around secret agents too long—needed a vacation more than she'd realized. She was starting to see menace in plastic dummies in store windows.

A banner stretching across the street from opposite light poles announced the coming of the Fourth of July parade. Three weeks away. Where had the year gone already?

Leaving the quiet streets of town, she wound her way through a tree-lined residential area and turned into the driveway of her grandmother's wood-and-brick house. Two strips of concrete represented the driveway. Untended grass growing along the center of the drive brushed the Cadillac's undercarriage. Behind the house, the detached garage loomed like a big old barn—with a padlock threaded through the hinge. Evidently, Grandma hadn't gotten around to installing the automatic garage door opener Penny had sent.

When she shut off the engine, silence pressed in on her. She was used to living on an isolated ranch, listening to the sounds of animals and insects and nature. She was used to being alone—or at least single. Tonight the quiet unnerved her.

She reached for her purse and got out of the car, digging through the bag as she went up the back porch steps. When her fingers didn't touch the set of keys she was certain she'd put there, she used a penlight to search the interior of the leather pocketbook, then ended up dumping the contents on the porch.

Great. She'd forgotten the darn keys the attorney had mailed to her. That wasn't like her. She was efficient to a fault—she had to be to run a highly secretive agency like Texas Confidential. Well, not exactly run it, but close to it. She was their right-hand woman—albeit behind the scenes. But all that was about to change.

Running her hands above the door and along the sides of the shutters, she searched for a spare key, knowing she wasn't likely to find one. Agnes Archer had been a private, paranoid woman. In a town where most people never locked their doors, Agnes had installed double dead bolts. She wouldn't have set out a spare key for some criminal to find.

Penny often wondered why her grandmother had been so fixated on criminals to begin with.

Unable to jimmy the windows that had been virtually painted shut over the years, Penny knew the only way she was going to get in and get any rest was to break a window. Going back to the car, she retrieved her tire iron and a blanket she kept in the trunk for emergencies.

Although she was prepared for the sound, she cringed as shattering glass rained inside against the pinewood floor. Wrapping her hand and arm in the blanket, she cleared the jagged edges away, then climbed through the opening onto the service porch.

Agnes had been gone for over two weeks now, but the clean, familiar scent of starch still lingered. The narrow beam of her flashlight passed over the ironing board sitting in the corner, the iron resting face down amid a rusty brown water stain.

Entering the kitchen, Penny slapped at the light switch, distressed when the power didn't come on. She was tired, her nerves rawer than she'd anticipated and she wasn't in the mood to stumble around in a dark house that evoked more emotions than she cared to feel.

Hoping it was just a burned-out bulb, she went into the living room and tried the lamp, knocking her shin against the end table and barely suppressing a curse.

When that light didn't come on either, she tried to recall where the circuit breaker panel was.

"Hold it right there."

Fear, primal and burning, stole her breath and shot through her blood with a dizzying jolt. For a fleeting, hysterical instant, her thought was that this was the wrong reaction for a government agent to have. Never mind that she wasn't a full-fledged agent yet. She should be deadly calm, ready to act and react.

Belatedly, though no more than a second could have passed, Penny whirled around, simultaneously shutting off the pitifully weak beam of the flashlight so as not to make herself a target. Her eyes not yet adjusted to the inky blackness, she crouched and reached for the gun in her purse. But before she could even register that her pocketbook wasn't hanging at her side, a shoulder slammed into her midsection and she went down hard, her hip jarring against the un-yielding hardwood floor.

Finesse gave way to sheer terror and self-preser-vation as she squirmed and kicked and jabbed. "You son of a—"

"Wait! Hold it..."

"Not a chance, buddy." She arched beneath her assailant. Unable to get good enough leverage to throw a decent punch, she started to bring her knee up.

"Hold on, wildcat...damn it...Penny, it's me."

He didn't have to identify who "me" was.

Memories flashed.

That voice. A voice she hadn't heard in sixteen years.

The voice of the only man she'd ever truly loved—or thought she'd loved—a man who'd made a fool out of her and broke her heart, a man who'd proved what her grandmother had spent nearly a lifetime drumming into Penny's head. That men were no good and not to be trusted with your heart.

Joe Colter.

Flat on her back, Penny hesitated in her wild struggle and it was distraction enough for Joe to get the upper hand. He manacled her wrists in one of his hands and jerked her arms above her head. With his free hand, he shined a flashlight in her eyes.

Penny was alternately stunned, confused and spitting mad. She bucked against him. ''Damn it, get the hell off me.''

From the flashlight's beam, she saw him grin. It wasn't fair that one man could be so handsome. Deep creases bracketed his mouth and fanned out beside his eyes.

''Not a chance.'' The repeat of her words seemed deliberate.

She went slack, her chest heaving with every breath she took, a combination of exertion, fear and much, much more. The weight of his body was beginning to arouse rather than restrain.

''Darby's welcoming committee, I presume?'' she finally asked, annoyed by the breathy hitch in her voice.

His grin kicked up another notch. ''Something like that. Although we're usually more mannerly.''

''I should hope so. You'll chase away the tourists.'' She took a steadying breath. ''It's been a long time, Joe.''

''So you *do* recognize me.''

She stiffened imperceptibly, then deliberately made herself relax. The last time they'd been together, they'd been in a very similar position. With him on top. And soon after that, she'd knocked the hell out of him with a right punch and walked out of his life.

"I recognize you. What are you doing skulking around my grandmother's house?"

"Protecting and serving."

"Good way to get yourself shot."

"Likewise—though I might point out that I'm still armed and you appear to be, uh, at a disadvantage, if you don't mind my saying so."

"Right now, I'm too tired to mind much. But I'll assure you, I'm only at a disadvantage because I'm allowing it."

His palm smoothed over her shoulder and down her arm, gently squeezing her biceps. She knew what he was feeling and resisted the urge to flex those muscles. Sleekly feminine, there was still power beneath that flesh. And the touch of Joe's hand was making it difficult to breathe.

"You're not gonna hit me if I let go, are you?"

Her lips curved. "Take a chance." When he released her wrists, her palm came up to rest on his chest, her fingers tracing the badge pinned there. "A lawman. I wouldn't have pictured it."

Joe rolled off her and reached for his hat that had been knocked off in the struggle. "Mmm, and you a secret agent. I wouldn't have pictured it."

"Who told you I was a secret agent?" She accepted the hand he held out and let him help her up.

"Your grandmother liked to brag. I'm sorry about her death, by the way."

"Thank you. I'm sorry I wasn't here for the funeral." Standing, she let go of his hand and rubbed at her hip, knowing she'd have a bruise. "I was out of town and by the time Kelly tracked me down, the funeral was over." Kelly Robertson had been Penny's high school friend and source of sporadic hometown information over the years.

Kelly had neglected to tell her that Joe Colter was still in town.

The last she'd heard, Joe had married and moved away. After gleaning that bit of information, Penny hadn't asked about him again.

It had hurt too much.

"Yeah. That's what she said." His tone was deep and gentle with compassion.

"You talked to Kelly about me?"

"Sure. Darby's still a small town."

Penny told herself she wouldn't cringe. Living in this small town—this gossipy small town—had caused the single most excruciating embarrassment in her life.

The moment when she'd realized that everyone but her knew that Joe Colter, the most popular jock in school, had seduced brainy Penny Archer on a bet.

And by God, she wasn't going to get caught up in all the old insecurities. It had been sixteen years. In the beginning, she'd convinced herself she hated him. She had to admit now that she didn't. The feelings were just as strong as they'd been the day after graduation.

And that scared her. Because it made her vulnerable. She hadn't thought of herself as vulnerable in a very long time.

"You okay?"

She clenched her fist and snapped her attention back to Joe. Or what she could see of him. "I'm fine. I'd be better with some light. Mind if I borrow your flashlight to find the breaker box?"

"I'll take care of it."

"Suit yourself. I think the panel's on the service porch. Careful of the glass."

She heard his boots scuff against the floor as he moved back through the kitchen, then heard the crunch of glass and the squeak of rusty hinges a second before the lights came on.

Turning in a circle, she glanced at the furniture— some pieces she remembered and some she didn't. There were changes here, but there was also familiarity.

She'd spent hours of her childhood in this room, yet scarcely a day of her adulthood. And that made her sad.

She looked up and saw Joe leaning against the doorjamb, watching her. He wore jeans and boots, a crisp tan uniform shirt with a badge pinned to his chest pocket and a tan Stetson hat.

A Texas lawman. Casual. Yet dangerous. He radiated welcome and power. And just the sight of him made her giddy.

The man was entirely too good-looking. Always had been.

She cleared her suddenly dry throat. "We both know how I got in the house. How did you get in?"

"Actually, I have a key. Got it from Reilly after Agnes passed away."

"The attorney. Is it just a coincidence, or is he the same Russ Reilly who played running back at Darby High?"

"The same. I'd have thought a woman with your connections would have checked out strange men sending you keys in the mail."

She arched a brow, feeling on more solid ground. She knew he was wondering about her and it felt good to be thought of as a woman of mystery. In school, she'd been brainy Archer, nobody special, someone who pretty much blended into the woodwork. Oh, she'd had plenty of friends—but few in the "in crowd"…except for Joe Colter. And courting that relationship had been a painful, lesson-learning mistake she would not repeat.

"Sounds like you're fishing for information, Colter."

"Maybe I am. All in the name of law enforcement, you understand."

She grinned, liking the feeling of keeping him off balance. She didn't normally play games with men. But then, she didn't normally come within touching distance of Joe Colter, either. "Then you'll understand about confidentiality."

"Mmm. What about professional courtesy?"

"I wasn't aware that we were on a case."

His gaze was very direct. "We could be."

Penny shivered. She didn't know when the conversation had taken such a turn, but she'd lost the thread. And had no idea what they were talking about or around, or what the innuendoes meant. She only knew that if she didn't get a grip, she was going to do something stupid. Like walk right into Joe Colter's arms and beg him to give her a refresher course on the feel of his lips against hers.

Or worse yet, to give *him* a refresher course, to show him exactly what he'd thrown away sixteen years ago, what he'd missed.

She took a breath, needed a distraction. "So...I heard you got married."

His nod was barely there, his gaze watchful. "Divorced four years ago."

A warm flush washed over her. "I hadn't heard that." Thinking he was married had been a buffer. Now that buffer was gone. And he was standing in front of her looking at her as though she was dinner. *Oh, man.* "Do you have children?"

He shook his head. "Wanted them. She didn't."

"I'm sorry."

"Me, too."

The hint of yearning in his tone connected with something inside Penny. Something she wasn't aware of and didn't understand. She shook off the odd tug.

"I'm surprised you stayed in Darby. I'd pictured you as a professional jock or corporate shark or something."

"I tried my hand at being an attorney and hated it. My heart's always been on the ranch."

"That uniform shirt and badge puts me more in

mind of a police officer than a cowboy—though the hat and boots beg a question.''

He grinned and tipped his hat. ''Police chief of Darby at your service. The mayor talked me into it. I divide my time between the ranch and town.''

''Busy man.''

''Makes me happy. You look really good, Pen.''

Penny resisted the urge to fuss with her hair and clothes. She did, however, stand a little taller. His gaze touched on her breasts, caressed everywhere they traveled.

Her gray T-shirt was snug, tucked into black jeans. She prided herself on being in shape, lifted weights and jogged to stay that way. Working in an environment with a bunch of men—highly trained agents— Penny felt the need to keep up, to maintain a lean, honed, healthy body. Now it was second nature to her. She liked looking good, knowing that even if she was wearing sensible, no-nonsense clothes, the body beneath was trim and toned and in good working order.

And seeing the appreciation in Joe Colter's eyes made her glad that she kept up.

''You're looking pretty good yourself, Colter.'' She moved past him and went into the kitchen. ''You on duty or would you like to stay for a cup of coffee?'' *Bad move, Archer.* But hospitality was ingrained in her.

''Actually, I'm off. One of the men was out sick so I worked a double shift and was on my way home when I saw your black Caddie pull into Agnes's driveway. I didn't know it was you.''

''And now you do.''

"And very glad of it."

His tone of voice made her shiver. She was not going to succumb to Joe Colter's charm. Giving the contents of the fridge a quick perusal, she said, "There's a can of decaf in here. Yes or no?"

"Sounds good." He hooked a boot around the rung of the kitchen chair, pulled it away from the table and sat.

Penny tried not to notice the breadth of his shoulders, or the way his presence filled the room. She tried not to remember how he'd looked sixteen years ago, sitting at this same kitchen table, algebra and English books spread in front of him, his dark brows endearingly drawn together in a frown of concentration. Back then, he'd still been big and masculine, but youth, she noticed, had given way nicely to maturity. Now, his presence felt totally different, dangerous somehow.

She was being ridiculous. She'd been living on a ranch with men for years, worked with men. Granted, recently there had been changes at the Smoking Barrel. Four of the agents had traded in their bachelorhood for happy marriage and family.

Maybe that's what was wrong with her. All the changes were setting her off balance, goosing her own biological clock.

But just because Joe Colter sat in her grandmother's kitchen oozing more sex appeal than was fair, was no reason for her to turn into a stammering, awkward girl. She was a much different woman than the one who'd left here sixteen years ago.

And she didn't intend to stay.

"You said you were on your way home, yet isn't this place a little out of the way? As I recall your ranch is the other direction." She filled the carafe with water and scooped coffee into the basket.

"The neighbors reported seeing a strange car outside a few days back. I've made it a point to cruise by since then."

"Wasn't me. I just got in."

"I know. I pretty much have my finger on the pulse of the town."

"Mmm, and that would be why you tackled me like a linebacker sacking the quarterback?"

He chuckled. "I didn't say my information was always accurate. I apologize for jumping you, but when a stranger crouches in a shooting stance, it's a natural reaction."

"I guess I'm lucky you didn't shoot first and ask questions later?"

"No, you're lucky I was the one who came to check rather than the Truman sisters. *They* would have shot first and questioned later."

Penny laughed. Though both women had been married—several times each—they were still known as the Truman sisters. Georgia was a retired telephone operator who knew the dirt on everyone in town, and Wanetta ran a dress shop in town that specialized in hats. As a child, Penny had wished the sisters could have adopted her. "Do they still live across the street?"

"Still. And believe me, your grandmother held you up to them like you were the President's guard.

You've become their hero, and it can get a little scary.''

Penny turned, feeling her heart soften. ''Grandma talked about me?''

''She was proud.''

''Why didn't she ever tell me? Why did she shut me down every time I called and wanted to visit?'' She asked the question aloud, even knowing Joe wouldn't have the answer.

''I didn't know you'd been interested in coming home.''

Snapping out of her inward thoughts, she looked at him. Censure colored his tone even though his features gave nothing away.

''You thought I'd just turned my back on her or something?''

He shrugged. ''Seemed that way.''

''As a lawman, you should know better than to assume. You ought to check your facts, Colter.'' Annoyed, she tapped her foot, staring at the coffeepot, wishing it would hurry up and drip. She was beginning to regret inviting Joe to stay.

''I don't imagine you're an easy woman to check facts on,'' he said reasonably. ''And I didn't think I had the right.''

She could have kicked herself. Her testiness made it seem like she cared what he thought of her, made it seem like she would have expected him to know her, to wonder about her, to keep up with her.

Those were her own fantasies. Not his.

The coffeepot wheezed and finally started pumping.

"So how long will you stay?"

She shrugged. "Long enough to get the house cleaned out and up for sale."

"A few weeks, then?"

"Yes, maybe a bit longer." Unless she ended up making a fool out of herself over Joe Colter.

"Need any help unloading your car?"

She shook her head, looked at him. "I can get it later."

"It's obvious you *can*." He pointedly glanced at the well-defined muscles in her arms. "Would you *like* the help?"

She swallowed hard at the look of appreciation shining out of his sexy eyes. "Ah, chivalry. Goes along with the protecting and serving, hmm?"

"You're nervous."

She nearly dropped the cup she'd been reaching for. Glancing over her shoulder, she did her best to appear bewildered by his observation. "Excuse me?"

"I'm making you nervous."

"You're being ridiculous."

"Am I?" he asked softly.

So softly, her hands trembled. She wouldn't melt, she told herself. She wouldn't fall into the depths of those intoxicating hazel eyes. "Yes. I've just driven over six hours. I'm punchy. Not nervous." Rather than waiting patiently for the coffee to brew, she took advantage of the pause feature and set her cup right under the drip mechanism.

"Whatever you say. You know you'll get a damn strong cup of coffee that way."

"I like it strong."

"What else do you like?" His voice was deep and provocative.

She laughed. "I'm not a pathetically naive girl anymore, and I'm not biting, Colter, so you can just rein in the flirting."

She didn't know he'd moved until he put his hand on her shoulder. She jerked and coffee hissed, spit and danced as it hit the hot plate.

"I think there's something we need to get out of the way." He reached around her to put the carafe back on the hot plate and took the mug out of her hand, then turned her to face him. "I owe you an apology."

She frowned. "For what?" He was so close she could feel the heat radiating from him. The urge to press against him had her heart pounding.

"For what I did to you. I know I'm late by sixteen years, but I wanted you to know how sorry I am for hurting you."

Penny was mortified that he'd actually brought up the subject and was thankful for the shadowy light in the kitchen—hoped it hid the immediate tinge of color that rushed to her cheeks. Color that might have been anger or embarrassment, she wasn't totally certain which. Probably a little of both.

Gathering her dignity, she ducked beneath his arm and moved away from him. "Really, Joe. Get over yourself. Do you actually believe I've given you a thought after all these years? I can't believe your ego."

He went very still. Similar to a panther watching his prey, waiting for the precise moment to pounce.

Danger radiated a second before he took his next step, crowding her against the cabinets.

And Penny found herself frozen in place.

"Haven't you?" he asked softly. "Thought of me?"

Since her tongue was stuck to the roof of her mouth, she shook her head.

"Liar." He put a finger under her chin, tipped it up. "Everything about you radiates a challenge, y'know that? And I never could resist a challenge."

She knew he was going to kiss her and she knew she should stop him. But she didn't do a damn thing to evade him.

His head lowered. A breath away from touching, he said, "I've thought about you. A lot. And I'd wager hard-earned money you've thought about me, too." His gaze dropped to her lips, moved back to her eyes. "Maybe this'll refresh your memory."

Chapter Two

I'd wager hard-earned money.

The words stung like bees around her heart, but her traitorous, needy body overruled common sense as she melted into the kiss.

His hips pinned her against the counter and his belt buckle pressed against her middle. For an instant she wondered why he didn't wear a thick holster with all the latest weaponry and gadgets, then remembered where they were. Darby, Texas. A little blip on the map outside of Austin. Here, there were no drug cartels or terrorists.

Just Joe Colter. The man by whom she'd judged every relationship over the years. The man who'd been her first love, who'd toyed with her affections and broken her heart.

The man who could still kiss like nobody's business. Just a minute longer, she told herself. Because she *had* thought of him. And she *did* remember. Oh, how she remembered.

But she couldn't allow herself to get caught up, to entertain any silly dreams or listen to mythical biological clocks ticking—a clock she intended to ignore, *had* to ignore.

Joe Colter was obviously entrenched in this town, the very town that she'd once run from—because of him. Her life was with Texas Confidential now.

Indulging a moment longer, her heart pumped when she felt Joe's fingers tremble as his hands gently framed her face. That she could cause the reaction in him filled her with feminine power.

As though a floodgate had suddenly been opened, she poured herself into the kiss—just to show him what he'd missed, she told herself.

The problem with cockiness was that it often backfired.

And Penny's intentions definitely backfired.

He insinuated a knee between her thighs, exerted just enough pressure to have her aching and throbbing and yearning to take him right down to the floor with her, to put out the fire.

And that was very dangerous. Joe Colter wasn't for her. He never had been and never would be. He made her vulnerable. And she'd spent the last sixteen years teaching herself *not* to be vulnerable—or at least how to hide it well.

She put a palm on his chest, eased back.

"Looks like you win the bet again."

He winced, closed his eyes and rested his forehead against hers. "I didn't mean—"

"I know." Why did she keep needling him in ways that reminded them both of the past? "Forget I brought it up. I participated as much as you did just now."

He leaned back and watched her for a long moment, looking as though he wanted to say more. Instead, he swept a finger beneath her eye. "You're tired. I shouldn't have taken advantage."

Gentleness. She wasn't used to it, and ridiculously, it made her want to cry.

Pretend, Penny. She deliberately let her gaze drift down the front of him, below his belt, then back up to his blazing hazel eyes. "From where I'm standing, looks like *I'm* the one who might have taken advantage."

His brow cocked. "You always did pack a hell of a punch. Both with your fist and with your mouth."

"Nice to know some things stay the same, hmm?"

"Or get better."

She saw the appreciation in his eyes. She knew she looked good, much better than she had as a nerdy high school girl. But beneath the makeup and casually provocative clothes, she was still no-nonsense Penny Archer. She hadn't been able to hold him sixteen years ago. She wasn't even going to try now.

"It's getting late…" she hedged.

"You're right. I'll find something to board up that window."

"That's not necessary. It's a warm night, I'll leave it for morning."

"The mosquitoes will likely carry you off by then."

She smiled. "I'll shut the kitchen door."

"It'll only take me a minute."

She let out a breath in a hiss. "I really am capable of boarding up—"

He winked, interrupted, "We aim to protect *and* serve."

"Fine, then. I'll help you."

"I didn't ask for help."

"Neither did I."

He shook his head and let out a sigh. "Why are you being so stubborn?"

"Oh, I don't know," she drawled, charmed despite herself. "Maybe because it's after midnight and I'm kind of tired? Or maybe because I'm just not used to being treated like a damsel in distress?"

"Baby, you don't look like any damsel in distress I've ever seen."

That made her laugh. "Compliments. I like those. Come on, Colter. Neither one of us'll get to bed if we don't take care of that window."

His grin was slow and provocative. "I think I'll leave that statement alone."

"Good idea."

They found a piece of plywood in the garage and hammered it over the opening. Joe insisted on helping her unload the car, too. He grinned when she glared at him.

"We're going to butt heads, you and I, aren't we?" he asked.

"Seems so. Are you looking for compliments to the mayor on how well you're doing your job?"

"Hell no. If I could hand this position over to somebody else tomorrow, I'd do it in a heartbeat."

That made her pause. "You aren't happy with your job?"

"I'd rather just run the ranch."

"Then why don't you?"

"I made a commitment."

Just like he'd made a commitment to seduce her all those years ago, she thought. Granted, it had been a bet, but he'd put his whole self into accomplishing the task. Boy, had he.

Penny hadn't realized just how much that incident still bugged her. She'd thought she'd dealt with it, matured, forgotten.

She hadn't.

She had an idea she was going to have to let Joe fully explain himself before she left. And she would tell him just how he'd made her feel, let him have it with both barrels. Get it off her chest.

Then she could move on.

Perhaps this was the unfinished business she'd thought about when she'd been driving into town. The part of her past she had to face and put behind her once and for all so she could move on.

But not tonight.

"Is that all of it?" Joe asked, setting down her duffel bag and handing her the case containing her laptop computer.

"For now." There was an attaché case in a special compartment of the trunk that held another weapon and more ammo, but she had an extra loaded clip for the thirty-eight in the suitcase. And chances of needing an arsenal in Darby were next to none.

She walked him through the house to the front door and held out her hand.

"It was good to see you again, Joe." He took her hand, staring at her with an enigmatic smile that made her want to squirm. His expression seemed to say that a handshake was pretty silly in view of that hot kiss they'd exchanged less than twenty minutes ago.

"Call if you need anything."

"Boxes."

"Boxes?"

"For packing my grandmother's things. Where would be a good place to find some?"

"Out in back of Garvey's market would be your best bet. The Evans just moved to a new place last week. I can check and see if they kept their packing boxes."

"No need. I've got to go into town tomorrow anyway. I appreciate the tip, though."

THE NEXT MORNING when Penny heard someone in the house she was prepared.

And deadly calm.

She palmed her thirty-eight and stealthily moved toward the kitchen. A drawer squeaked, wood binding against wood. A utensil clattered against the floor.

Knife?

Adrenaline jolted like a shot of pure caffeine. A hell of a noisy intruder.

Gun palmed upward, back against the wall, Penny took a steadying breath, pivoted and crouched in an offensive stance in the kitchen doorway.

She swore when she saw Joe retrieving a fork from the floor.

Her thumb shot the gun's safety home and her finger came off the trigger.

"Damn it. Don't you know about doorbells and such?"

He turned, looked from the gun in her hands to her face.

"I knocked. You didn't answer. And you left the door unlocked, by the way." He pulled fragrant rolls out of a bag. The coffeepot was already hissing and spitting steam as water dripped through the grounds. The smell alone was enough to make her forgive him.

But he was still staring. "Good way to get yourself shot," she muttered as she ducked and looked at her reflection in the toaster. She nearly screamed.

What resembled a distorted, four-eyed raccoon stared back at her. Great. Behind the lenses of her glasses, mascara was smudged beneath her eyes. It wasn't until she heard Joe groan that she looked down and belatedly realized she wasn't dressed.

The little camisole and tap pants covered all the essential parts—barely. Emerald satin, they were designed to evoke sensuality, for both the wearer and the admirer.

And Joe Colter was definitely admiring. A bit dumbstruck if one wanted to get right down to it.

A brazen sense of feminine power swept her, had her shoulders pulling back despite the glasses and messy eye makeup.

His gaze finally lifted back to hers. "Coffee?"

She nodded and took the mug he held out to her. With the gun in one hand and the coffee in the other, she couldn't make any gestures of modesty. Nor could she wipe away the smudged mascara. And despite the appreciation in Joe's eyes, she felt the need for a more even playing field, a bit more armor.

"If you'll excuse me a moment, I'll put on something a bit more suited to company."

"Don't go to any trouble on my part."

"Wouldn't dream of it."

JOE FINALLY TOOK a breath when Penny left the room. The satin hem of her little underwear things barely covered the well-toned swell of her behind.

He was going to have major daydreams. And night dreams too.

Penny Archer had changed. Confident, sexy, with just a bare hint of vulnerability that lurked beneath the surface. A vulnerability she did her utmost to hide. He was trained to pick up on subtle nuances. And he'd picked up on hers.

He wanted to pick up a lot more.

But Joe had already been through a rough time with relationships. He had no business entertaining fantasies about a woman from his past. He'd hurt her once. And he didn't want to hurt her again.

What did he have to offer that she could possibly need? She obviously had an exciting position as a government agent—though exactly what type of an agent he wasn't sure. Regardless, she wasn't likely to give that up for small-time life on a ranch.

Because ranching was Joe's goal. Not law enforcement, or power lunches or good versus evil. He just wanted to be himself. Please himself.

And engaging in a temporary relationship with

Penny Archer would be no better than what he'd done to her sixteen years ago.

But man alive, he wanted to follow her into that bedroom and run his hands over that satin encased, dynamite body. She intrigued the hell out of him.

When she came back in the kitchen, she wasn't wearing her glasses. She'd cleaned up the smudges from beneath her eyes, enhanced them a bit with shadow and added a pale gloss to her lips, making them look wet and tempting. Her curly hair was held off her neck with a clip, the style casual and haphazard and sexy as all get out. The snug jeans and even snugger tank top outlined every delicious curve of her body.

There was an innate sensuality that radiated from her like a shiny gold coin beneath an icy brook, yet there was an aura of mystery, too.

She met his gaze and held it, quietly, comfortably, directly, as though she were a totally open book, a woman of sophistication and experience.

But Joe had an idea few people really knew a damn thing about this woman.

She broke eye contact and looked at the white bakery sack. "Are those Danish from Ellie's bakery?"

"The same."

Penny pounced. "Coffee and Ellie's rolls. You're a handy man to have around, Joe."

He grinned. "Not many can resist Ellie's goodies."

"And you exploit that weakness to get you off the hook for breaking and entering, hmm?" She bit into a sugary cinnamon bun, closed her eyes, and moaned. "Heaven."

Joe swallowed hard. A fleck of powdered sugar clung to the gloss on her bottom lip. Mesmerized, he dragged his gaze away from that temptation.

"It wasn't breaking and entering. The door was unlocked, remember?"

"So you say." She took another bite. "I thought Rosa was a great cook. I'd forgotten about Ellie's delights."

"Rosa?"

"The cook on the ranch where I live."

Joe realized there was a lot he didn't know about Penny. "You live on a ranch?"

"Yes. And I love it."

"Enough to give up being a secret agent?"

She frowned at the odd question. "Don't need to. The ranch is my home and my home base."

He had no idea what possessed him to ask such a question in the first place. And though he truly wanted her to tell him more, her evasive tone and look told him today wouldn't be the day.

Evidently, his interrogating skills were getting rusty. Then again, Penny Archer hadn't committed a crime. He had no reason to interrogate her.

Except for his own personal enlightenment.

"So, other than taking your life in your hands, what are you doing here?" she asked.

"Bringing you coffee and rolls...and boxes."

"Oh. Thank you." She looked around the kitchen. "There's a lot to sift through. I'm not looking forward to it."

He moved closer, touched her smooth cheek, could

practically feel her battling to stand her ground, to keep from flinching and stepping back.

She didn't trust him. That was clearly evident.

"Can I help?" *Speed up the process that'll take you out of my life again?*

She shrugged, rubbed a palm against the thigh of her jeans and stepped around him. She did it smoothly, nonchalantly. He knew she wasn't as composed as she wanted to appear.

"I imagine it'll just be tedious stuff. And between keeping the peace in town and tending to cattle or whatever on your ranch, I can't picture you having a whole lot of spare time."

"I have competent officers in town and a foreman and full crew on the ranch. I wouldn't mind spending time with you, Penny. Catching up."

"I don't know if that's such a good idea, Joe—"

"Yoo-hoo! Anybody home?"

Penny smiled, felt her insides go all fluttery. She knew that voice. Georgia Truman. One of the honorary aunts from across the street. Wanetta couldn't be far behind.

"Aunt Georgia," Penny said, meeting the women in the front hall where they'd already let themselves in the house. "And Aunt Wanetta. It's so good to see you." She hugged each woman.

"Land sakes, let's have a look at you," Georgia said, holding Penny at arm's length. "Look, Wanetta. Our girl's all grown up and she's got muscles. Didn't I tell you that job of hers was demanding?"

"Yes, you did, Georgia," Wanetta said, adjusting

the netted hat she wore that had been knocked askew when Penny had hugged her.

"We saw Chief Colter's car out front and thought we ought to get over and make sure you're not having troubles."

"No, nothing like that. He brought coffee and some of Ellie's rolls."

"Ah, yes, you poor dear. Of course you don't have proper food and supplies in the house. Agnes would have ousted us from the bridge club if she'd known we waited so long to be hospitable like this."

"You're forgiven. I just got in last night. And it was very late." Penny smiled, feeling a little overwhelmed. She wasn't prepared for the emotions that took over at the familiar sight of the women she'd always wished were kin rather than mere neighbors.

Just as she wasn't prepared for her emotions over Joe.

It really would be in her best interest to get out of town as quickly as possible. But in the light of day, getting a good look at her surroundings, she realized how much her grandmother had let the house run down. It would take some fixing up to get it in shape to sell.

"Oh, Netta and I heard you come in. But we saw Joe's car then, too." She paused just a beat. "We didn't want to come over in our nightclothes with a man present and all. What I meant was we shouldn't have waited so long this morning."

"If you'd been earlier, you would have caught *me* in my nightclothes."

"And very nice ones at that," Joe commented softly.

Georgia and Wanetta exchanged a pleased look and Penny glared at Joe. "Don't you have work to do? Criminals to catch?"

"Darlin', your window breaking is the most exciting criminal-type activity that has happened around here in a while." He winked. "But you're right. I am due to clock in."

"Someone broke your window?" Wanetta asked.

"I did. I forgot Grandmother's key."

"Oh, what a pity. Although we couldn't have been much help to you there. We gave Agnes a spare set of keys to our house, but she never would reciprocate. Wanetta and I figured you'd probably written her some telling letters, and she felt concerned she might compromise our government's secrets if some old snoop read the wrong correspondence."

"Not that she ever came right out and called Georgia or me a snoop," Wanetta added, the netting on her hat bobbing like a wiry feather duster.

"I'm sure she didn't." But Penny was feeling sick to her stomach, now. She hadn't written lengthy letters to her grandmother. Oh, she'd sent Christmas, birthday, and various holiday cards, added a few lines of personal tidbits. Out of courtesy and duty. Out of guilt.

But Agnes had never reciprocated. And the few times Penny had called, suggested a visit, Agnes had discouraged it.

So why had her grandmother obviously bragged?

Why had she led the neighbors and townspeople to believe their relationship was a loving, confiding one?

It was like the behavior of someone whose relative was a social misfit. Lie, brag and pretend to outsiders lest they find out that person's offspring isn't quite up to snuff.

Like they'd all done with Penny's mother.

Was that it? Did Agnes fear Penny would end up like Jeanice Archer? Had she been insulating herself against potential shame?

"Oh, dear," Georgia said. "We've made you sad. Agnes was a strange old bird, but she was your grandmother and I'm sure you miss her."

"Yes." Startled, Penny looked back when Joe moved next to her, placed a palm on her shoulder and squeezed.

She wished he'd keep his distance. And that he wouldn't touch her. It would be all over town before lunch that she and Joe had a thing going.

A rumor spread innocently. Not maliciously. But still too close to the past for comfort. The sisters would mention Joe and Penny's name in the same breath and the gossip mill would take it from there.

She moved out of his reach. "Thank you for bringing breakfast and the boxes, Joe."

"My pleasure." He tipped his hat, gave her that reckless smile that told her he knew he was being politely kicked out. "My offer still stands to help out."

"I'll be fine. But I appreciate it."

He went down the porch steps and Penny noticed how the wood bowed and nails were popping up. The railing between the brick posts holding up the roof overhang were sagging and weather-beaten. This house was a mess.

"Still a handsome devil, don't you think?" Georgia said.

Penny nodded before she realized Georgia had addressed her question to Wanetta. A sneaky ploy.

"Y'all come into the kitchen and I'll see if there are any tea bags."

"Oh, there are. We had a meeting here for the school board a couple of days before Agnes keeled over with the bad heart. She served a divine coffee cake and an assortment of flavored teas. All very classy."

For Christmas, Penny had sent her grandmother a collection of gourmet tea, along with a pot and an antique china cup-and-saucer collection. She'd imagined her grandmother leaving it in the box on a shelf somewhere.

But according to Georgia and Wanetta, Agnes had used the gift proudly. Entertaining the school board.

"Why did the school board meet here?"

"Agnes was a member. Darnedest thing. After grouching at and scaring half the children in the neighborhood, she suddenly developed a soft spot for them—though she did her best to hide it. Even started a fund-raiser to benefit orphaned children."

"That's nice." Penny set water on to boil and didn't turn around. She didn't want the neighbors to see how stunned she was. And hurt, perhaps. Penny herself had basically been an orphan. Her father had been around, but not often, and not for long periods of time.

And though Agnes had taken her in, given her food and shelter, she'd never made Penny feel welcome.

Agnes Archer had tried her best to teach Penny that she was unlovable.

Chapter Three

Remembering Joe's subtle censure over her not being here for the funeral, Penny wondered if Georgia and Wanetta were thinking the same way.

She turned, looked at the two old women. "I would have visited, but Grandmother always made up excuses and told me not to."

"Oh, we know that, dear."

"You do?"

"Of course. Agnes was a pill—more often than not had her lips all puckered up like she was gonna spit. Not many folks understood what made her tick." Georgia laughed and waved a hand. "I like to think I've got an edge on most, being a retired telephone operator and all."

Penny felt a smile grow. The aunts could always put her at ease. "Aunt Georgia, you're not going to tell me you eavesdropped on private conversations, are you?"

"Of course I'm not going to *tell* you that, darlin'." Her sly smile said it for her.

Besides, everyone in town knew exactly how Georgia had gotten so much of her information.

Penny poured tea in cups, put the rest of the bakery rolls on a plate in the center of the table, and sat down.

"Just like you didn't *tell* anyone that Stan Saffrone kept a place over in Austin—and had built a real nice swimming pool over his dead wife's body?"

Georgia sniffed and tugged at her polyester vest. "I can't imagine how anyone could draw a parallel between a telephone operator and a typed note left on the police department's front desk."

"Of course not," Penny said with a grin. "Must be my suspicious mind."

"And well you should have a suspicious mind. That's an asset to a spy, I'd say. You must regale us with some of your exciting stories, dear."

"Now, Aunt Georgia…" The telephone rang, saving her. Penny rose to answer, frowning when no one responded. "Hello?" she repeated. Unwilling to play the game, she disconnected first and turned to face the neighbor ladies who were both staring with rapt, expectant expressions.

"The grapevine must work fast," Penny said with a soft laugh. "Too bad whoever it was didn't have the courage to speak."

"Did you get a heavy breather?"

"No. Just didn't want to talk. Probably the wrong number…unless Grandmother had a special friend?" She didn't think that likely, but it wouldn't be unheard of. Someone pining for a lost loved one, dialing a familiar number in a moment of weakness, hoping against hope that death had been a dream, a big mistake.

"Agnes had friends, but no one close. Up until the very last she pretty much held us all at arm's length," Georgia said, staring at the telephone receiver Penny had already replaced in its cradle.

"And folks in Darby don't just hang up," she continued. "Wrong numbers are simply a good reason to visit with someone new." She sent a look at Wanetta. "Press automatic call-back and let's see who it was."

"Aunt Georgia, if someone's trying to get in touch with me, they'll try again."

"We did have us a case of a heavy breather a month or so back. Old Dudly Ferring got a drunken obsession with Thelma Croft, but she blew a whistle in his ear and burst his eardrum, so I don't imagine he's at it again this soon."

"Nope. No heavy breathing."

"Suppose one of your spy cases has found out you're here?" Wanetta asked.

"Wanetta, I do believe you might be on to something." Georgia lowered her voice dramatically. "Are you in danger, dear? Because Wanetta and I can bring over the shotguns and stand guard."

Penny laughed and held up her hands. "No shotguns, Aunt Georgia! I'm not in danger. I promise."

"Well, if you were, you know you could count on us. We take care of our own here in Darby. But of course you'll remember that, won't you dear?"

Penny remembered. Though she didn't feel like *she'd* been lovingly taken care of. At least not by her grandmother.

Now the sisters, on the other hand, had gone a long way to filling the emotional gap. They'd wanted to lynch Joe when he'd hurt her. Actually, they'd wanted to string up Joe's father, Cyrus Colter, who Georgia claimed was a useless son of a gun who wanted to live his life through his son and constantly pushed Joe when a smarter man would have known to ease up.

Penny reached across and gave both Georgia's and Wanetta's hands a squeeze. "It's so good to see you both again. I wish I'd just ignored Grandmother's cold shoulder and come home anyway."

Wanetta adjusted her ridiculous hat. "You're here now, that's what matters. We'll have plenty of time to catch up. But we'll not hog all of your time. I'm sure you'd like to see some girlfriends."

"I'd planned to stop by Kelly Robertson's." After she made a trip to the cemetery.

"Ah, yes. You know Kelly's opening a bookstore, don't you?"

"Mmm. She'd said so in her Christmas card."

"Due to have the grand opening next week. She'll be so happy that you're here to attend. Let me just jot down the telephone numbers for you—although you can get them through information. Folks hardly ever go to the trouble to have their numbers unlisted—especially now with those caller ID features."

Georgia rummaged through one of the kitchen drawers, found a scrap of paper and scribbled numbers.

"This'll save you getting caught by Loralie Vanna. She's one of the local operators here in Darby. She's supposed to use the computer, but she's so nosy, half the time she butts right in and engages folks in conversation. I've a mind to report her to her superiors, but Wanetta reminds me it's not my job anymore. Runs my blood pressure up. Here you go, hon.'' She handed the paper to Penny and gave her a hug.

''Come for supper if you want,'' Wanetta said. ''Georgia's got a chicken all ready to fry up, and there'll be plenty. Maybe we can even talk Joe into stopping by. A single man, and all, he could use a good home-cooked meal.''

Penny kissed the honorary aunts on the cheeks. ''Thanks for the invitation, but don't count on me. I've got a ton of things to do, and I can't promise a time when I'll be free.''

''That's fine, dear. The invitation stands—anytime.''

When the sisters left, Penny called Kelly to let her friend know she'd be by later for a visit. Hanging up, she couldn't help thinking about the other phone call.

For no good reason, Penny got an uneasy feeling. She'd heard a series of subtle clicks on the line, like the skip of a tape recorder. But why would anyone call and record her voice?

Just to be on the safe side, Penny figured she ought to send a gently probing e-mail to Kendra at the Smoking Barrel. Just to see if anything unusual was up at Texas Confidential headquarters that she should know about.

KELLY ROBERTSON had hardly changed a bit. Still bubbly, outgoing and friendly. She'd put on a little weight after three kids, but it sat well on her, made her look like a woman. Happy and healthy.

"My gosh," Kelly said when she opened the door. "You look fabulous!" Two shrieking little boys charged past, nearly knocking Penny off the porch. Tightening her grip around the two-year-old in her arm, Kelly made a grab for the little hellions and missed. "Sorry. Come in. Come in. Boys! Stay in the yard."

"Okay, Mom!"

Kelly shook her head. "I love getting your cards every year. I can't believe it's been twelve years since I've actually *seen* you!" Twelve years since her father's funeral and Mitchell's invitation to come work for him. "Janelle and Pam are still griping because you didn't come to the reunion."

No, she hadn't come back for the reunion. She'd been worried that Joe would be there. And as much as she might have liked to flaunt her success and hard-won independence, she hadn't trusted herself to be strong.

Penny stepped into the house, hugged Kelly, and smiled at the little girl who promptly latched onto a hunk of her curly hair. "Ouch!" she teased.

"Makayla, quit it," Kelly admonished the baby gently, disentangling the fat little fingers. "You don't pull the hair of important government ladies."

"Get out," Penny said.

Kelly laughed. "Yeah. Can't get too mysterious for me. I know your secrets."

"If you remind me about that strawberry wine incident, I might have to deck you."

"Looks like you could mop the floor with me easy enough." She tested Penny's firm arms. "You make me sick,'' she said fondly. ''Here you are all sleek and sexy and I'm a dumpy mother of three.''

''You're not dumpy and you're much more than just a mother—although that's a fine profession in itself.'' Unaccountably, Penny had the urge to hold her hands out to little Makayla, to see if the baby would come to her. Weird. ''I'm anxious to see your new bookstore.''

''Oh, you will. But not today, okay? I've about stocked and inventoried myself to death. Today's play day. Girls' day. I hope you don't mind, but I called Pam and Janelle and told them you were coming. They ought to be here any minute now. I hope that's okay?''

''Sure. I'm dying to see everybody.'' The doorbell rang. ''Speak of the devils?''

''Yes. Brace yourself,'' Kelly said. ''It's about to look like an unruly day-care center in here.''

Without waiting for an invitation, the door opened and Janelle and Pam came in, each juggling children. The women squealed, set down their kids and ran to hug Penny.

''You dog!'' Pam said with a laugh. ''Look at you. Miss Secret Agent, herself.''

''Who told everybody I was a secret agent?'' Penny asked.

''Oh,'' Janelle said. ''I just *knew* that was supposed to be hush-hush. Your grandmother said something at the beauty shop, and I was booked solid that day— seemed like the whole town was there. That must have been five or six years back.'' She gave an apologetic shrug and rested her hand on the shelf of her pregnant belly. "By now, I don't imagine there's a soul in Darby who doesn't know."

They went into the kitchen. Amid coffee cups, baby bottles, little boys running through the back door tracking sand and dirt, toy trucks scattered under the table and a miniature pink shopping cart being shoved repeatedly against the cabinet—and nobody batting an eye or checking for damage—the room was absolute chaos.

And Penny felt a jolt of longing and envy so strong she nearly doubled over with it. Here were her friends. Girlfriends. Girls who'd cried over boys, failed tests, and whined over having to wear stretched out swimsuits in gym class. Penny, it seemed, had always gotten the ones worn by the seniors with gazonga boobs. Her firm little lemons had fared pitifully beneath all that sagging material.

"Russ said if I saw you before he did to tell you he has some papers for you to sign," Pam said. "Russ was Agnes's attorney—but you probably already know that."

"Yes," Penny said. "I'd planned to stop by, but to be honest, I'm procrastinating. Grandmother's house is in pretty bad shape and I don't really know where to start. So I decided to take the day off, catch up with y'all and bring in some groceries. And honestly, how is it you're having conversations with your husband over breakfast about me when I've just got into town?"

"It wasn't over breakfast. Right after Kelly called to say you were coming over, I phoned Russ so he'd know where I'd be if he needed me. Actually, I was angling for him to take the day off and baby-sit, but no such luck.''

''Speaking of everybody taking the day off,'' Janelle said. ''I could open up the shop and we could all run over there and do hair and nails and primp. I operate a beauty shop out of my house now. Not that you look like you need to primp,'' she amended quickly. ''You've got the most gorgeous skin. I always hated that about you. Here I am with all the freckles and you don't have a one.''

''Your freckles are cute,'' Penny said. Kelly had written about Janelle's troubles. She'd finally divorced her no good husband who'd drank and caroused and abused her. Penny was glad to know Janelle had opened her own beauty shop. ''And your little girl's the spitting image of you.''

''Her name's Lindsey.'' Janelle smiled at the shy six-year-old. ''She seems a bit awestruck by you.''

Penny laughed. ''Why? Did you tell her I was someone scary?''

''No, *I* did,'' Pam said. ''Not scary. I told her you were a James Bond girl.''

''Oh, no,'' Penny groaned.

''Don't worry,'' Kelly said. ''Janelle doesn't let Lindsey watch R-rated movies so she doesn't have any idea what a James Bond girl is. But you could always enlighten us,'' she invited slyly.

''Oh, yes,'' Pam said. ''Tell us something juicy.'' The three women looked at Penny expectantly. Lindsey shyly inched forward to stand by Penny's chair. Baby Makayla was still ramming her pink shopping cart into the cabinet.

"It's not all that glamorous. I work for a branch of the government that handles sensitive cases—which, unfortunately, I can't speak about."

"Penny!" Pam wailed. "You can't just leave it at that." Her voice lowered and she leaned in closer across the table. "Have you ever shot anybody?"

Penny rolled her eyes and glanced pointedly at Lindsey.

Janelle added her own censoring glare at her friend, then said, "Lindsey, hon, would you redirect Makayla from that cabinet before she knocks a hole in it? Take her on out to the front room where there's more area to maneuver."

"Okay." Lindsey immediately jumped to obey her mother. No whining or sass. Penny wondered if the girl's shyness and lack of obstinence came from having lived with an abusive father. That thought made her sad. Penny knew about living in a household where you felt the need to walk on eggshells.

When Lindsey had herded Makayla out of the room, Kelly poured another round of coffee. "So, *have* you shot anyone?" she asked ghoulishly.

"Yes," Penny said, deliberately shocking her three friends. Well, she *had* winged one of the cattle rustlers a few months back.

"Oh, my gosh!" Pam cried. "I was sure you'd say no. Is it okay for us to know this? I mean, I don't have to keep quiet around Russ or anything, do I?"

Penny's smile grew cunning. "Since I'm sort of Russ's client, he has a certain loyalty to me, don't you think?"

All three women were looking at her with awe. "Did you kill the guy?" Kelly asked.

"No. The object is to bring them in alive."

"Seems silly," Janelle said softly, almost to herself. "If you could rid the world of some of its vermin then they wouldn't be taking up space in our jails…and becoming eligible for parole."

Penny reached over and squeezed Janelle's hand. From Kelly's letters she'd learned that Janelle had pressed charges against her ex-husband, Don Gilard, and had sent him to jail for abuse. "I'm really sorry for what you had to go through, Nelle."

Janelle squeezed back. "Thanks, Pen. I'm happy now, though. I married Jim Edwards, a really sexy, shy guy. He loves Lindsey to pieces and we're expecting this one in late September." She patted her swollen tummy.

"Good for you. I'm anxious to meet him."

"Oh, you will," Kelly said. "Since he's my accountant, he'll be at the bookstore opening next week making sure I'm handling my assets properly. But you should come to the fair tonight. It's the last night before they pack up and leave town. We're all taking the kids and dragging the hubbies along, too."

"I don't know," Penny said. "I've got an awful lot to do."

"You said you were procrastinating and playing hooky today. Start tomorrow on your grandmother's stuff. In fact, I'll come help you."

"No. You've got your bookstore to deal with. And I'll need a couple of days at least just to figure out what's what at the house. I'll mostly be spinning my wheels, I imagine.''

"So, meet us at the fair," Pam said. "You were always the daring one on the roller coasters and vomit rides. We'll make you take our kids.''

"Oh, that's just what she needs," Kelly said. "Kids hanging on her back pocket. You ladies forget she's our resident celebrity.''

"Get out of here," Penny said. "Why in the world would you call me a celebrity?''

"Do you see anybody else coming back to town with this much excitement and mystery surrounding them? Dine on it, baby.''

"I'm not mysterious.''

"So pretend, for goodness sake. Lanie Dubois will be pea green with jealousy. She still thinks she's better than anybody else. Do you know she actually showed up at the reunion with her pom-poms? Acting all cutsie and lording it over everybody else that her daddy was promoting her to Vice President of the bank—and of course telling us she didn't *have* to work, but wanted to contribute something worthwhile to society.''

"Yeah," Pam added. "She tried to make us feel like a bunch of house frumps.''

"You're kidding." Kelly and Janelle were business owners and Pam ran a small ranch, sat on just about every charity board imaginable, and sold real estate on the side. Added to that, all three were raising children.

House frumps? Not likely.

"So what do you want me to do? Wear my thirty-eight on my hip?"

"Can you?" Kelly asked, rubbing her hands together.

Penny laughed. "No. And don't you all start with me. I'd just as soon keep a low profile while I'm here, okay?"

"Killjoy," Pam said. "Once Joe Colter gets a look at you, low profile will be history. He's as visible as they come and he'll set his sights on you in a heartbeat."

"Don't even go there," Penny said, making a great effort to keep her voice even and her smile pleasant. "Guys like Joe Colter just don't do it for me anymore."

She was lying through her teeth.

A quick glance at Kelly confirmed that her friend saw right through the lie. Kelly was the only one who knew that Penny had actually slept with Joe Colter. The rest of the town just thought he'd dated her on a bet. A charity case, so to speak.

Only Kelly knew the whole truth. That sixteen years ago, she'd given her virginity and her heart to Joe Colter—and neither one had meant a thing to him.

THE WARM JUNE AIR was redolent with the smell of popcorn, hot dogs, peanuts and cooking fires. Music played and children shrieked.

Carrying a cone of blue cotton candy, Penny walked around the fair grounds, smiling at folks who kept looking at her like they ought to know her but couldn't quite place her.

For now, she didn't go out of her way to introduce herself. She was content for the moment to let the memories pour over her, memories of other fairs here in Darby, fairs she, Kelly, Janelle and Pam had attended as girls.

Long, banquet-style tables draped with paper cloths were set up in the middle of a makeshift food court where booths emanated wonderful scents of both American and ethnic fare. The lights on the huge Ferris wheel lit the sky with neon colors. Screaming children rocked the top gondolas as the wheel slowly stopped and started, loading and unloading riders. Calliope music from the carousel vied with the dings and bangs of ringtoss and shooting booths. The Octopus and Tilt-a-whirl had long lines of children and adults waiting their turn to become walking candidates for chiropractic healthcare.

Off in the distance, the clack of roller-coaster cars climbing the grade then speeding around dips and curves called to her.

Penny loved roller coasters. She loved danger. The faster and scarier, the better.

Tossing her cotton candy cone in a trash barrel, she stopped at one of the food booths and ordered a beer.

"Hello stranger."

Penny jolted and nearly spilled the paper cup of beer.

Joe, wearing his hat and an apron over his uniform shirt was serving up barbecue spareribs, slaw and corn.

His gaze raked her from head to foot, his eyes

alight with pure male appreciation. "I saw the cotton candy. Did you decide it's time for dinner, now?"

Penny made a deliberate effort to steady her nerves. "Hey, life's short. We should all eat dessert first."

"And keep a body like that?"

"Good genes," she said and felt a pang. She didn't come from good genes. In fact, there was a horrible, secret flaw in hers. But she wasn't going to think about that now. "I thought you'd be out keeping the peace. How'd you end up with barbecue duty?"

"The mayor roped me into it. Said it was good-will."

"Doggone mayor must be some persuasive guy. Just talks you into all sorts of things, huh?"

"Seems that way." His grin was that of a good sport. No one looking at Joe Colter would ever make the mistake of thinking he was a man who could be pushed around. He made his own choices. Perhaps some of them were governed by the wants and needs of others, but ultimately, it was his decision. "You here alone?"

"Yes. I'm looking for some friends."

"Kelly, Pam and Janelle."

She raised her brows. "Is there anything that gets by you?"

"Not much." He pointed with his industrial size spatula. "Table over there in the corner by the pizza stand. They just got here a few minutes ago."

"Thanks. I'll go join them."

"Want a plate of ribs to go?"

"Sure." She unsnapped the small purse clipped to her belt, reached for her wallet.

"On the house," Joe said.

"Whose house?"

"Mine. I donated the beef."

"Isn't the money going to a charity?"

"Yes. A women's shelter."

"Then—"

"Take the plate, Archer. I'll donate a few extra bucks just in your honor."

She grinned and put away her wallet, accepting the paper plate he held out to her. "Such a deal. The shelter and I thank you."

With her heart still pumping over unexpectedly seeing Joe and trying her best to hide the trembling in her hands, she turned and wove her way through the tables.

Joe Colter was definitely going to be a distraction while she was here.

When she got to her friends' table, she simply grinned, nodded and sat down to eat. Pam was mopping up spilled coke, Janelle was trying and failing to tie a suitable bow in her daughter's hair, and Kelly was at war with her sons. Penny was thoroughly entertained.

"Please, mommy. I want to do the Thunder Rider," ten-year-old Justin complained.

"Me, too," Kevin said, putting his hands on his hips.

Penny licked her fingers and gave the little boy a wink. "Tough guy."

"We already talked about this, boys," Kelly said. "No big rides tonight. Daddy's not coming until later and there's nobody to go with you. Besides, you've just eaten. You'll get sick.''

''No we won't.''

''Yeah, Mom,'' Penny butted in. ''No, we won't.''

Kelly glared at her. ''Real cute, girlfriend.''

''Do you object to the ride for safety reasons, or do you just not want the boys to go alone?''

''The rides are safe—they've ridden them every single night for the past three nights. I just don't like them to go alone.''

''Then, I'll take them.''

''You just ate half a plate of barbecue.''

''So?''

''Yeah, so?'' Justin and Kevin chimed in.

''Fine,'' Kelly said. ''It's your stomach and whiplash.''

Penny grinned. ''My stomach's cast iron. Who's going on Thunder Rider?''

A chorus of ''me'' sounded.

AS IT TURNED OUT, Penny ended up with Kelly's two boys, Justin and Kevin, and one of Pam's sons, Kyle. Steven was too young, Pam said, and earned herself a four-year-old with heartbroken tears tracking down his face.

''Honestly, Steven,'' Pam admonished. ''We've been through this every night.''

''But I'm older tonight.''

''Kid's got a point,'' Penny said only loud enough for Pam to hear. She knelt down in front of little Steven. ''How are you at target practice, buddy?''

He sniffed and shrugged, but his round blue eyes brightened.

"Tell you what. Soon as we get back, I'll take you over to the shoot-'em-up booth and we'll win the biggest prize they've got. Okay?"

"'Kay." Steven shot his brother and friends a "so there" look and everyone ended up happy.

"What about you, Lindsey?" Penny asked. "Want to come?"

"I'll stay with Steven," she said quietly. Shyly. Something about this child spoke to Penny. Lindsey reminded Penny a lot of herself at that age. Quiet and withdrawn.

Don't act ugly, Penny, or your crazy mother will act even uglier. And then what, huh? Everyone will know just what hideous stock you come from.

She shook off the memory, passed a hand over Lindsey's straight-as-a-board hair. "Promise to ride on the Ferris wheel with me? We can take Steven on that one, what do you say?"

Lindsey's eyes came instantly alive, then she composed herself quickly. "Yes, ma'am. I'd like that."

Penny met Janelle's gaze. Sadness was there, a parent's heartache when she knew the cause of hurt and was trying her best to fix it, but couldn't seem to make a lot of headway.

"She'll snap out of it," Penny said to Janelle as she walked past. "Though I could clobber you for teaching her such good manners. I *hate* being called ma'am. Come on guys."

After a turn on the Octopus, the Tilt-a-Whirl and two passes on Thunder Rider, Penny rendezvoused with Lindsey and Steven for the promised ride on the Ferris wheel and trip to the shooting booth. The kids were treating her like a favored aunt they'd known all their lives and Penny was having a ball.

Now, watching them as their energy wound down and as her girlfriends danced with their husbands who'd finally shown up, Penny felt something inside her crack with longing. She was thirty-four years old and the ticking of her biological clock was nearly deafening.

But children weren't for her. The risk of passing along a horrific flaw was too great.

Her hips and shoulders gently moved to the rhythm of the country-and-western ballad the band was playing. Feeling like a fifth wheel since everyone else seemed to have a husband to hold on to, Penny turned to leave.

A hand at her shoulder and warm breath at her ear stopped her cold.

"Care to dance, secret agent lady?"

Excitement and dread sent a shot of adrenaline through her system.

No, she answered silently. This was a bad idea. A very bad idea.

But Joe didn't give her a chance to accept or object. He simply swept her into his arms and onto the make-shift dance floor before she had sense enough to decide on her own.

"I didn't say—"

"Shh," he whispered against her temple. "Just keep moving your hips like you were a minute ago. I'll follow."

She started to object, laughed instead. "Still the same old smooth-talkin' Joe."

He pulled back slightly to look at her. The move caused their lower bodies to press. Penny drew in a breath, tried to act sophisticated.

"I'm not the same kid I was at eighteen."

Penny really didn't want to take this trip down memory lane. If she did, she'd likely give herself away. All her tough-girl talk about never even giving the incident or him a second thought would be exposed for the pitiful lie that it was.

Still, she couldn't help the dig. "And I'm not the naive eighteen-year-old that I was, either."

"I can vouch for that." His palm smoothed over her back, from her shoulders to the top of her hips, finally settling at her waist. "I want to ask you if we can be friends. But honest to God, Pen, all I can think about is being much, much more than friends."

She looked into his eyes, licked her lips. It would be so easy to kiss him right now. If she leaned forward just a couple of inches...

The friction of the front of their bodies was fairly causing sparks.

Her heart pounded.

Get a grip.

Her chest rose and fell against his as she took a deep cleansing breath, then rested her cheek on his shoulder.

"Dance, Chief. I'm not staying in town long enough for us to think about 'more.'"

Chapter Four

Together they swayed to the music, a sultry ballad that seemed to evoke a sensual mood that Penny wasn't prepared for. She didn't usually feel small and feminine around men—she normally made it a point to hide her femininity. But with Joe, she was a different person.

His shoulders were wide, his chest firm against hers. He surrounded her, towered over her, made her feel cherished.

Just like he had those last months before high school graduation.

"I can hear your mind turning. You're thinking about much more than dancing."

So what was a little harmless flirtation? she asked herself. She leaned back just a bit. The brim of his hat nearly touched her forehead as he gazed down at her. "You're a potent man, Joe."

"Then we make a good match."

Her fingers tightened on his shoulder. At one time she'd truly thought they were a great match. She shouldn't ask. She did anyway. "Why did you do it?"

The entreaty in her eyes must have supplied what her words didn't, because he immediately understood the question.

"I never meant to hurt you. When I asked you to tutor me, that's all it was. Just the jock asking the class brain to give him an extra edge, get me through finals. But I started to look forward to our time together." He ran his hand up her back, beneath her hair and cupped her neck. His gaze dropped to her mouth.

"Don't," she said, glancing around at the other couples dancing.

He held her close when she would have pulled away. "Easy. You started this, so hear me out."

"I'm listening. That doesn't mean I'd like a repeat of history where I'm the center of the gossip mill. And if you keep looking at me like I'm dessert, that's exactly what's going to happen."

"I hate to tell you this, but you're already the center of the gossip mill. You're our mystery lady."

"I prefer mystery lady to poor Penny, the butt of the joke. Or the bet."

Joe felt his gut tighten. By rote, his feet moved to the music, but his mind focused on a time he wished he could rewrite.

"Did you ever think to ask if I was in on the bet?"

"Joe, the whole town was talking about—"

"Except for me."

"You weren't...you didn't...?"

"No." He felt her heart pound, felt the perspiration cling to her palm. "There was a bet. But I wasn't part of it."

"Damn it, Joe. You could have said something."

"When? As I recall, I was pretty busy picking gravel out of my teeth after you'd slugged me. And by that time, my pride was smarting."

"Still—"

"You meant a lot to me, Pen," he interrupted softly. "And that scared the hell out of me. It would have been so easy to lose myself in you. And I'd already given so much of myself away to everybody else. The coach was pushing me to carry the team, my folks were pushing me to be the best and get a scholarship. You and I didn't move in the same circles, but when the guys found out I was spending time with you, they made a big deal out of it."

His hand tightened at her waist. "I didn't take the bet, Penny," he said again. "You should have known me better."

"Based on one weekend?"

"There was more to us than a weekend of sex." Although he had to admit, that was the single, most vivid memory in his life. When he'd made love with Penny, she'd rocked his world. He hadn't expected the feelings. Hadn't been prepared.

They'd spent one glorious weekend at the lake. Penny had told her grandmother she was staying at a friend's house. He'd told his dad he was fishing with the guys. In a rented cabin they'd spent forty-eight hours nearly killing each other trying to sate the flashpoint desire that had grabbed them by the throat and wouldn't let go.

Beneath the glasses, plain features and simple haircut, Penny Archer had been a tigress in bed. But even more than that, she hadn't expected him to be the big man on campus, hadn't cared if he could throw a football or wondered if he intended to make something of himself after school.

She'd just wanted him for himself.

And it had been the greatest aphrodisiac.

And then she'd come to school on Monday morning, sought him out when he was standing with a bunch of his friends. It was obvious by the look on her face and the familiar way she'd smiled at him, waited for him to take her hand, put his arm around her, that she fully expected him to announce to his buddies that they were a couple.

It was a reasonable assumption.

He'd been a stupid jerk. He'd hesitated.

And his friends had pounced. *"Hell, he actually did it. Way to go, Colter. Pay up guys."*

Penny had immediately read between the lines, formed an instant, negative impression by his hesitation. *"A bet?"* she'd asked, her brown eyes so filled with pain even now he remembered. Then she'd laughed, squared her shoulders and sucker punched him right in the jaw.

"Your actions didn't give me much encouragement that our time spent together had any depth," she said, bringing his mind back to the present.

"And neither did yours. You made a snap judgment. I was a stupid kid who needed approval. Yes, I hesitated. Maybe I wanted you to give me more credit."

Penny looked into his sincere, hazel eyes, then sighed and rested her cheek on his shoulder. "I understand what it's like to need approval, Joe. I tried to get it from my grandmother for years.'' Had that caused her to be unreasonably unbending? What if she'd stayed and let Joe explain? Set aside her insecurities? Sixteen years was way too late for what-ifs. ''But everyone knew we'd been at the lake together. What did you tell them?''

''That you wouldn't sleep with me.''

''Get real. No teenage boy admits sexual failure like that.''

His palm came around her rib cage, his thumb brushing a path of fire scant inches from the side of her breast.

''I did. And after you damn near knocked me out in front of them, they believed it. Respected you, too.''

''Oh, they did not.''

''Yes they did. Russ Reilly said if I didn't go after you for real, he was going to make a play himself.''

Penny was astonished. ''Pam's Russ Reilly? My attorney?''

''One and the same. I decked him.''

Penny laughed. ''I take it you've mended fences?''

''Yeah. Though we still have a friendly rivalry going. My department arrests people and Russ gets them off.'' He gazed at a point over Penny's shoulder. ''Except for Janelle's scum of an ex. Russ refused to take the case, did everything he could to help the prosecution send the guy to jail.''

Penny looked around, saw Janelle dancing with her husband, Jim. He had one arm around her waist, a hand resting protectively at the side of her pregnant tummy, and in his other arm, he held Lindsey. "Janelle seemed worried that Don might be up for parole."

"It's been granted. I just found out late this afternoon. I still have to tell Janelle and Jim. God, I hate to do that. She was so messed up for a while, and that little girl of hers has been through the mill. Jim's been great for them. I just hope like hell that Gilard doesn't show his face in my town once he's out."

My town. Another reminder that this was where Joe belonged. And though Joe's explanation of the bet soothed her ego some, it didn't change the fact that the timing was still off for them. It seemed it always would be.

The music ended and they stood on the grassy earth, looked at one another. "If he does show up, call me and I'll be your backup."

Joe grinned. "I like the sound of that. Want to come to work for me?"

"In your dreams, Colter." She moved out of the dancing crowd and Joe followed. "I'm through playing second fiddle. Now ask me to run the joint," she teased, "and I might just give it some thought."

"Careful what you offer. I'm planning to retire in a few months."

"Gonna be a cowboy?"

"It's what I'm happiest doing."

And he looked every inch the cowboy, too. An outlaw cowboy. Her heart thumped and she knew she needed a distraction. They were passing the shooting booth, and Penny stopped. "Want me to win you a stuffed animal?"

His hazel eyes narrowed as he looked down at her. "Why do I get the feeling you and I are going to spend a great deal of time on one-upmanship?"

"Maybe because you're a perceptive guy?"

"I happen to be the chief." He left out the "of police" part as though elevating himself to the town father or something. Penny hid a grin and nearly rolled her eyes.

"And I happen to be the best," he continued. "I've won the Darby shooting competition four years in a row. I'd hate to ruin your 007 mystique by showing you up."

She smothered a laugh. "How do you manage to carry that huge ego around?"

He grinned. "I manage." Reaching in his pocket, he took out his wallet. "Give us two rounds, Farell," he said to the man behind the booth.

"You sure about that, Chief?"

Joe's brows drew into a frown. He glared.

Farell shrugged and handed Joe a twenty-two caliber rifle loaded with blanks. "It's your reputation."

"Wise guy," he muttered. He turned to hand the rifle to Penny, and noticed a crowd was starting to gather.

"Place your bets, folks," Farell called. "And I tell you, my money's on the James Bond gal. I already seen her shoot. Durn near cleaned me out already."

Joe glanced quickly at Penny to see how she'd reacted to the bet comment. They'd just had an uneasy conversation about this very thing. He didn't want to make her feel uncomfortable again.

She squeezed his arm, her sassy smile telling him

that she was okay with this particular bet. The light of challenge in her eyes made his heart stutter.

"I just might toss my own ante into the pool," she said.

"Talk about egos," he muttered. He tried to press the rifle in her hands, but Penny shook her head.

"I challenged you, remember?"

"I remember you offered to win me a stuffed animal. Ladies before gentlemen."

She still shook her head, liking the calculation and appreciation she could see in his eyes. With a laugh in her voice she said, "Oh, no. Chief before agent. I've got rank so it's my call."

"Hey, you go, girl," Kelly said from behind her. Penny noticed that her three friends and their husbands had gathered in a cheering section. She reached back and shook hands with Kelly's husband, Tom Robertson, and Pam's husband, Russ Reilly. "It's good to see you guys again." Then she held her hand out to Janelle's new husband. "Jim Edwards, right?"

The accountant nodded. "Nice to meet you."

"Same goes. You're just in time to see me cream the golden boy, here."

"Mommy, can I bet, too?" Justin Robertson asked.

"No, you may not," Kelly said to her son.

"Aw, man. Easy money. Penny's gonna wipe him out."

"You know, I'm starting to feel just a touch inferior, here," Joe complained. "Where's all my town support?"

"Right behind you, pal," Russ said. "But if she

shoots half as good as she punches, my money's on Penny. Sorry.''

''Pressure,'' Joe said good-naturedly. He hefted the rifle to his shoulder. Metal silhouettes of ducks, rabbits, bears and birds moved side to side, some going straight, some popping up at random, then disappearing.

Twenty shots, rapid fire. So far he was doing well. The ammo was pinging and silhouettes were disappearing. Suddenly a silhouette of an old woman holding a basket popped up. If he shot her he'd lose all his points. Penny saw Joe's finger flinch. He didn't shoot the tin civilian. But the distraction was enough to cause him to miss the bear that popped up next.

Penny knew she was gloating, but she couldn't seem to help herself. And clearly, by the look on his face, Joe thought she was bluffing about her own abilities.

''Nice try,'' she said with false commiseration and accepted the gun he held out. ''Shame you missed the biggest animal out of the bunch.''

Regardless of whether or not Joe had actually accepted the bet sixteen years ago, this small town had ears and knew everything that went on. She'd left here with people thinking she was pitiful Penny and that Joe would only date her on a bet.

She'd be darned if she'd let anybody underestimate her again.

Hands steady, she lifted the rifle to her right shoulder, closed her left eye, sighted.

''Deadeye,'' Joe murmured, moving close, dipping his knees to sight over her shoulder.

She paused, glanced at him. "Do you mind? I gave you room."

"Yeah," he said softly, so softly only she could hear him. "But your perfume didn't. It distracted me. Cocoa butter and coconut. Like an exotic island girl. I've carried that memory for a lot of years."

Darn him. Her insides turned to mush and began to tremble. She elbowed him in the chest. Took a breath. She couldn't smell any perfume. If he thought she'd ask for a handicap, he had another think coming.

She steadied the gun again. Focus.

The calliope music and motor of the Ferris wheel faded into the background. It was just her and the silhouettes and the site on the gun. She'd done this thousands of times during target practice, done it for real when confronted with drug lords posing as cattle rustlers. With a gun, she could hold her own with any man.

Joe held his breath. He knew he'd gotten to her, yet here she stood, steady as a rock. Brown, shoulder length hair, curling wildly, blew against her cheeks. Her flawless skin glowed with perspiration from the warm June night. Beneath her taut skin, her biceps flexed, as did the muscle in her forearm as her finger squeezed the trigger twenty times in rapid succession. Twenty plinks and downed silhouettes followed the rifle's report.

He was impressed and proud and so turned on it took everything within him not to snatch her to him and cover those full, smiling lips with his.

"Told ya," Farell said. "I'm gonna have to ban

her from my booth. She'll clean me out of animals. What's your pleasure, sweet thing?''

She pointed to a floppy-eared donkey, accepted it from Farell and held it out to Joe.

''A donkey?'' he asked, grinning. ''Are you trying to say something about my behavior?''

She smacked the animal against his solar plexus and he had no choice but to grab it.

Laughing, she said, ''Well, if the shoe fits…but actually, cowboy, I chose it because it was the closest thing to a horse I saw.''

His insides softened as his hands tightened around the animal. She'd appeared to choose at random, but her choice had meaning. She cared about his dream. And won him a gift that represented that dream.

He wanted to return the favor. And much, much more.

But her girlfriends were around her now, congratulating her, gloating with her. He grinned and stepped back. He could take the teasing.

''Okay, okay,'' Russ said to his wife. ''We've embarrassed Joe enough for one day. Let the guy have some peace. And we need to get going.''

''Thanks, buddy,'' Joe said, though he really didn't need anyone sticking up for him. His ego and masculinity weren't smarting as he'd teasingly made it appear. Besides, he appreciated competitiveness. From a male or a female.

When their friends left, Joe asked, ''Want to go somewhere and get a drink. Or coffee and pie?''

Penny shook her head. ''I'm all done in. I should be getting home.''

"You'll start going through your grandmother's things tomorrow?"

"Yes."

"Will it be hard on you?"

"Probably. Despite the circumstances, I cared. It's hard to go back there and know that she's gone."

"Then let me come home with you."

She went very still. Was he asking for more?

With the backs of his knuckles, he brushed her cheek. "Just to talk. I don't want the evening to end."

"I think it's best if it does, Joe." Absolutely the best. Because Penny's willpower was on very dangerous ground where she and Joe were concerned.

She wasn't staying in Darby.

And allowing herself another intimate taste of Joe—which is exactly where she knew they'd be headed if they kept this up—was pure folly. The memories would haunt her forever.

JOE WATCHED HER walk away, watched her get in that sleek black Cadillac with its darkened windows. Even her car was sexy and mysterious.

The urge to follow her home was almost more than he could resist. He admired her. Was intrigued by her. Damn it, he wanted a second chance with her.

She wasn't a woman who would bend easily, yet despite that tough-girl persona, she could be hurt. He knew that only too well. If he could, he'd spend a lifetime atoning for that hurt.

But he'd rather spend that lifetime discovering all her secrets. Having her stand by his side. Walk with him. Talk with him. Ride with him. Make love with him.

He had an idea Penny Archer was his soul mate.

But destiny had put them on different paths.

And right now, those paths were only crossing temporarily. Life's road would turn again soon. She'd go her way and he'd stay on his.

Unless he could somehow change her mind. She'd cared about him once. Could she care again?

He had to find out. This time it would be her choice. He would tell the world he was pursuing Penny Archer.

THE NEXT MORNING, Penny decided she was still in procrastination mode. It was the craziest thing. She never procrastinated. She was efficient to a fault.

She'd gotten as far as dragging out some boxes that held photographs and odds and ends, but the little collie panting happily on her front porch and looking like he'd been rolling in a mud puddle had snagged her attention.

She'd checked for tags, asked Georgia and Wanetta if they recognized the dog, and when they told her the pooch was a stray, Penny gave him a bath, fed him and took him to the vet to have the tear on his ear looked at. She couldn't just let the poor thing wander around eating out of the trash cans. If an owner didn't turn up during the time she was here, she'd take him back to the Smoking Barrel ranch and let him live out his days there. Heaven knows there was plenty of room.

And Penny kind of liked the idea of having a little

company while she was here. Maybe a pet would ease this sudden, ridiculous, impossible notion she'd gotten about having children.

And wanting to make love with Joe.

Returning from town with a carload of dog supplies, she glanced at the honey-gold collie. "You can be my pretend kid. What do you say, boy?"

The dog barked. Penny pulled the Cadillac into the driveway, distracted by the handsome man leaning against the porch railing. Blond hair, nice build, slacks and a polo shirt. Not a cowboy. She automatically glanced around for a vehicle and license plate numbers. The plates were Texas, but the car had a rental company sticker on the bumper.

"Is that your owner, boy?" she asked the dog, feeling her heart sink. The collie panted over her shoulder, licked her face then scrambled to get out once she'd opened the door. He ran, tail wagging, to the front porch where their visitor squatted down to greet him.

Penny followed. "Hi," she said. "Is that your dog?"

His blond brows rose. "I hope not since he just got out of your car. That'd make you a dognapper."

She smiled. "I might be one of those anyway. I found him this morning on my porch. I thought maybe you'd come to claim him. Since that's not the case, can I help you with something?"

He stood and held out his hand. "My name's Nathan Lantrelle. I'm looking for Agnes Archer."

"My grandmother passed away three weeks ago."

"Oh. I'm sorry." He reached out and touched her

arm, removing his hand before the contact could make her uncomfortable.

"Did you know my grandmother?"

"No. But my grandfather did. I know this is going to seem like a crazy, really awkward question, but are your parents around?"

"No." Penny simply left it at that. She wasn't sure if he was coming on to her, trying to make her feel young. A typical salesman trait. She was very good at getting information, without giving any—or very little—in return.

"The reason I ask is a bit touchy. But I've come all this way, so I may as well tell you my story—or our grandparents' story in this case. If you want to toss me out on my ear, that's fine."

Their grandparents' story? Well, that was fairly intriguing.

"I can at least offer you a glass of lemonade before I do any tossing." She smiled and gestured to the wicker porch furniture with its faded blue cushions. "Would you like to have a seat?"

"Yes, thank you."

He played with the dog while she went in and filled icy glasses with tart lemonade. Returning, she sat in a chair angled slightly toward the love seat both he and the collie were now occupying.

"I guess nobody's trained him to be a watchdog," she said, noting the happy expression on the dog's face. "He appears to be quite the social mutt."

"Dogs are drawn to me. I've got two Irish setters. My mom's watching them for me right now."

"That's nice." A man who had a good relationship

with his mom and animals. That was a plus. "So where are you from?"

"Houston."

"And you said you were looking for my grandmother?"

"Yes, I wanted to meet her." He paused, drew a folded piece of paper out of his wallet, held it out to her. "Here. This will probably explain much better than I ever could. My grandfather was in love with your grandmother. They were engaged at one time, but he made a dumb mistake and left her standing at the altar. He regretted it, but...well read the letter. You'll see."

Penny accepted the paper that was creased and yellowed with age. Why was her life suddenly deluged with men bent on atoning for past mistakes? The words were printed in ink, the letters small and well formed. Grandma would have needed a magnifying glass to read them.

She started to skim, then went back and feasted on every agonized word, touched despite her skepticism. This was clearly a love letter. That in itself astonished Penny. Given her grandmother's disposition, she couldn't imagine a man writing such poetry.

Yet it truly was poetry. He spoke of her body, her skin, the way her eyes had softened for him, the way he imagined those same eyes had filled with pain when she'd found herself waiting alone in a church filled with people. He spoke of a young man controlled by wealthy parents, a young man who'd made the wrong choice and had regretted it almost immediately.

Just when Penny was about to look up and ask a question of Nathan, the next sentence caught her attention.

My darling Agnes.

I'm dying now and must accept that I'll never again look upon your sweet face, but I had to let you know that not a day has gone by that I have not remembered you, yearned for you, and regretted terribly the hurt I caused you. I've written you so many love letters—even when I wasn't free to do so—but you've returned them all. That is why I have asked my grandson, Nathan Lantrelle, to deliver this one in person. If I'm to go to my grave, I must have peace in my heart that you know I loved you. That I love you still. Please forgive me.

Penny swallowed hard, and her hands actually shook. "My gosh, I had no idea. My grandmother was a...a difficult, unhappy person. To know that someone felt this way about her..."

"Perhaps she was unhappy due to my grandfather's treatment."

"For that many years?" *Well think about it, Penny. You're still mooning over Joe.*

Nathan shrugged. "Obviously she married—as did my grandfather."

"Yes, she married." And that man, Penny's grandfather, had abandoned her, too. Penny was starting to see her grandmother's life in a different light.

She knew only too well about the pain of putting

your hopes in a man and, rightly or wrongly, having them dashed.

That's why it was best to pursue an exciting career. Not a man.

"I'm sorry I missed meeting her," Nathan said. "My grandmother has been gone awhile, and Gramps was alone when he died. He talked to me about Agnes. She was the woman whose name was on his lips when he slipped away, even though he'd been married half his life to someone else. It wasn't just my promise to deliver the letter that motivated me. I truly wanted to meet the woman who'd had such a profound and lasting effect on Gramps." He gave the dog a scratch behind the ears, grinned. "Although looking at Agnes's granddaughter, I can begin to *see* why."

Oh, he was very smooth. And very handsome. Too bad he didn't make her heart go pitty-pat. "Thank you."

"So, what'll you do now that she's gone? I assume you'll be living here?"

"No. As soon as I go through my grandmother's things, I'll put the house on the market."

"Sell a great old house like this?"

"Yes. I don't live in Darby."

He smiled. "Yet you take in stray dogs."

"Looks like *you* ought to be the one to take him in."

"Animals love me. Guess that shows I can't be all bad, huh?"

What an odd thing to mention. "Did someone say that you were?"

He laughed. "No. I think that was my clumsy attempt to put you at ease, perhaps get you to consider going out to dinner with me. Would you? Consider it, I mean.''

''I hardly know you.''

''Which would be the purpose of a meal. To remedy that.''

''Then perhaps I might consider it. But not tonight,'' she said gently. She liked the way he was looking at her. With interest. It gave her feminine self-assurance a boost. She hadn't had much luck in the romance department lately. And though Nathan didn't make her heart pump or her stomach flip, he was a handsome man. It was a nice compliment.

He stood and the collie hopped down off the cushions, trotting over to sit at Penny's feet. ''See there,'' Nathan said. ''He's a good host, but his loyalties are with you.''

''I don't even know his name.''

''So give him one. Call him Al. After my grandfather.''

Penny smiled, doubting she'd take the advice. The collie just didn't look like an ''Al'' to her. ''I'll come up with something.''

''Well, it was nice meeting you…hell, we've shared love letters, refreshments and a proposal for a date, but I don't even know *your* name.'' He grinned.

''Penny.''

He took her hand in both of his. It was a deliberate, telling action, especially when he held on for several seconds longer than was polite, and gave a squeeze.

''It was very nice to meet you, Penny. I'll be around for a while. If you happen to come across anything from my grandfather, keepsakes or letters

Agnes might have written him..." His words trailed off.

"I'll let you know. Where will you be staying?"

"I'm not sure yet. I just got here." His gaze skittered away, yet his features were arranged in a perfectly open expression. Penny got the distinct impression he was waiting to see if she'd invite him to bunk on her couch. He'd delivered his message—albeit three weeks late and to the wrong Archer woman. Odd that he'd decide to stick around.

Penny wondered if she was being too suspicious. If she didn't watch it, she'd become as cynical as her grandmother had been. Clearly, Nathan was attracted to her. In that case, most men would take a few days to see if they'd get lucky.

She could have saved him the trouble, but her ego urged her to just let it be.

"I think there's a motel eight miles or so outside of town."

"Thanks, I'll check it out." He hesitated. "You know, since we're practically family and all..." He grinned and shrugged apologetically for the lame line. "I could help you pack up. Haul stuff down from the attic. Give you free use of my muscles and we could reminisce about our respective grandparents in the meantime. By then surely you'd feel comfortable enough to go out with me?"

She'd gotten more offers to help her sift through her grandmother's belongings than she could shake a stick at.

"Thanks just the same, but at this point, I think I'll make quicker progress by myself." From the corner of her eye, she saw the squad car pull up at the curb, saw Joe get out. The curtains across the street at Georgia and Wanetta's house twitched again.

Penny controlled her smile. Both of the aunts had been in and out of the house four times since Nathan had arrived—or rather since Penny had arrived and found him on her porch step. They'd come out to water the geraniums, check the mailbox, snatch up a weed in the flower bed, and for reasons that were beyond Penny, Wanetta had come out with the broom and given the bird feeder hanging in the tree a couple of whacks. Maybe the seeds had been stuck together. Seemed a good stir with the finger would have done the trick as well or better than a whack of the broom. Each time they'd come out for a quick, seemingly specific reason, then waved and retreated back in the house.

"I'll take a rain check on that dinner date, then," Nathan said. He stepped off the porch and nodded to Joe as the men passed each other on the walkway.

Joe stopped in front of her.

"Good afternoon, Chief."

"Archer."

She grinned. "The aunts called you, didn't they?"

"They take their neighborhood watch seriously." He glanced back to the car pulling away from the curb. "Friend of yours?"

She bit her lips to keep from laughing. His tone was a touch surly. Joe Colter jealous? Imagine.

Chapter Five

"Would you like to come in for refreshments, Chief? You look a little...hot under the collar."

His smile was slow and predatory as he advanced, mounting the porch steps. He stopped at eye level with her, crowding her.

She refused to step back, held her ground, even though it cost her.

"Yeah, I could go for something...or *someone*." He wrapped his hands around her hip bones, urged her backward and came up the last step, forcing her to have to look up at him.

It was a deliberately provocative move.

And it made Penny tremble.

He grinned and his gaze dipped to her lips, the brim of his Stetson nearly touching her forehead. "You're not looking quite so cool now, Archer."

"It's ninety degrees out, for heaven's sake. Get a grip, would you?" She stepped back and his hands dropped away. "And what's with you cruising around in a patrol car at all hours? Don't men in your position rule from an office or something?"

"Not in Darby. Everybody pulls their weight."

"Well, maybe you should go pull it somewhere else."

"Do I make you nervous?"

He'd asked her that before. She started to lie. Changed her mind. "Yes."

His brows lifted, shifting his hat. "Then we're making progress."

"I didn't know we'd lost ground."

"Sixteen years worth."

She shook her head. "We're not picking up where we left off, Joe. Too much water under the bridge. Too much growth."

"No. Not where we left off. A different place, I think. A better place."

She took a breath. "I don't think I'm ready for this conversation."

"Sure you are."

"Fine. Let me restate. I don't think I *want* to have this conversation."

With a finger, he tipped up her chin, studied her eyes. "Sure you do."

She licked her lips, felt them twitch, felt a smile grow. "You're so full of yourself."

"That's part of my charm."

"Well, do you want to bring your charm inside before Georgia and Wanetta have heart attacks, or do you have to get back to work?"

"What exactly are you offering?"

She laughed. "Not what you're thinking, buddy. Lemonade and air-conditioning. Take it or leave it."

"I'll take it. For now."

She ignored the taunt and preceded him in the

house, nearly tripping over the collie who darted in ahead of her.

"Whose dog?" he asked, stopping in the front room while she continued on into the kitchen.

"Beats me. I found him this morning looking like a refugee from a flood zone, so I cleaned him up and ran him over to the vet's office to see about his torn ear." She got down more glasses and took the pitcher of lemonade out of the fridge. "Doc gave me some salve for his ear and pronounced him healthy but hungry. So far nobody seems to know where he belongs. Do you?" she asked, returning to the living room.

"Haven't seen him before."

"Then I guess I'll let him hang around with me for a while." She handed Joe a glass, nearly dropped it when their fingers brushed. She cleared her throat, looked down at the collie. "I should probably come up with a name for him. Nathan suggested I call him Al, but that doesn't seem to fit."

"Nathan?"

She took a breath, decided she was steady. "The guy you just passed. Turns out his grandfather—*Al*—and my grandmother had a fling."

"That's a new one."

"New what?"

"Pick-up line."

She laughed. "Are you jealous, Colter?"

"Damn right."

That took some of the wind out of her sails. Because by the look on his face, he was dead serious. "Well…um, that's nice."

"So, this Nathan person just stopped by to tell a

perfect stranger that his grandfather was your grand-mother's lover?''

''No. He came to see grandmother, to deliver a letter to her. He didn't know she'd passed away.''

''Oh.''

''See there. Now don't you feel bad for thinking suspicious thoughts?''

''Not a bit.''

Penny swallowed hard and sat down on the sofa. Joe was different today. More intense. More…determined. The collie came over and lay at her feet. ''What do you think about Scout?''

''Excuse me?''

''For the dog's name.''

''Kind of like an agent in training, hmm?''

Penny laughed. ''I doubt he'd make a good agent. He's too friendly.''

''You're pretty friendly,'' Joe pointed out, sitting down beside her on the couch. ''Does that make you a bad agent?''

It didn't make her *any* agent. Yet. ''We're talking about the dog, Joe.''

''I'd rather talk about you.'' His gaze traveled like a sensual caress from her hair, to her snug tank top, down to her shorts. Stunning her, he reached over and hooked a hand around her calf, lifted her bare foot to his knee and massaged her toes. Amusement lit his eyes. ''Scout suits him fine. Your sandal seems to suit him, too.''

Penny jerked her foot back and snatched her sandal from out of the dog's mouth. ''Shame on you, Scout. I rescue you from a life on the mean streets and you repay me by eating my shoes.'' She'd kicked them off as soon as she'd sat down. She was on vacation, she told herself. After years of dressing smartly every day, she deserved to be a little casual.

''I like the red polish on your toes. Makes your skin look really sexy.''

Penny figured she was going to have to lower the thermostat on the air conditioner. She was way too hot. She hopped up from the sofa, slipping her feet in her sandals, then snagged a packing box and a stack of old newspapers and went to tackle the contents of the maple wood china cabinet.

Hoping her voice didn't betray her nerves, she said, ''This sexy skin needs to get busy. It'll be time for me to go back to work and I won't have accomplished a thing.''

''You enjoy your job?''

She paused in the act of wrapping a cup and saucer. She'd decided to keep the Desert Rose patterned china. If she ended up relocating to the Montana branch of the Confidential Agency after her training, she'd likely be setting up her own housekeeping after all these years living at the Smoking Barrel among someone else's belongings. ''Yes, I enjoy it very much.''

''You never did say what exactly it is that you do.''

''No,'' she said softly, evasively. ''I didn't.''

He stood, came toward her. She put down the china before she dropped it.

''You know, that mysterious aura really gets to me. Intrigues the hell out of me, if you want to know the truth.'' He stopped in front of her, touched her cheek.

"And if I wasn't mysterious, then what? If I blended in with the woodwork, would you still be intrigued?" She had no business asking that question. But she couldn't help it. This wasn't her normal mode of dress. He was responding to an outer package she'd deliberately enhanced with cosmetics and figure-hugging, provocative clothes. Oh, sure she wore sexy underwear daily—that was her one indulgence. But other than that, in her normal life, she was pretty much a no-nonsense, no frills woman. Plain, even.

"Baby, you couldn't blend in with the woodwork if you tried." His head started to lower.

She put her fingers against his lips, met the desire in his eyes. She knew her own eyes reflected the same emotion.

But today would not be the day to indulge.

"I'm not who you think I am, Joe."

"Who do I think you are?"

She frowned, her brain muddled, shook her head.

"Do you know how sexy it is when you get those little lines right there between your brows?" He ran a finger over the slight creases. "You're always so quick. But every once in a while, something throws you for a loop. I love watching you try to sort through it."

The corner of her mouth tipped up. "So you're deliberately trying to provoke me into premature wrinkling?"

He smiled at her, ran a thumb over her jaw. "We've got quite a bit in common, you and I."

She raised a brow. "Like?"

"We're both in law enforcement…so to speak."

"So to speak," she agreed, meeting his watchful stare. He wanted information she wasn't at liberty to give him.

"We both have a grandparent who left us a house in Darby."

"Your circle C's a bit more than a house—what, about a thousand acres more?"

"Nine hundred and eighty-six."

She rolled her eyes. "Let's split hairs while we're at it."

He grinned. "I really do like you, Pen."

And I really do love you.

The renegade thought burst in her head like the clang of a breached security alarm. Her heart lurched and her throat closed. Oh, no. Surely not. Not after all these years.

Shaken to her very core, she stepped out of reach, turned and began to pack the china. "So, how are your parents?" she asked, willing her insides to steady.

"Dad's slowing down. It worries me some. That's why I'm planning to retire. The time's right for me to pick up the slack on the ranch." He took a stack of plates down from the cabinet and began wrapping them in newspaper. "Mom's still the same. Cooks up a storm, gives riding lessons at the ranch and teaches a painting class over at the community center."

She'd met Joe's parents a few times when she'd gone to his ranch to tutor him. His father had been boisterous, a bit pushy, but a man who loved a good joke and loved to tease. His mother was beautiful, quiet…so serene and normal. She was the epitome of motherhood. For a girl whose own mother had been horribly dysfunctional, Penny had been filled with both envy and awe, had absorbed each nuance and imagined what it must be like to live that way—in a completely normal family unit.

"What's the matter with your dad?"

"Rheumatoid arthritis. He still gets out of bed every morning, drags himself up on a horse, but he's in a lot of pain. I keep telling him to take mom and go someplace. Have a vacation, a rest. Let somebody else take care of them for a change, wait on them. God knows, they've got the money. They could travel for the next twenty years and still be fine."

"Well that's impressive."

"Gramps struck oil about ten years ago," he explained.

"And left you all in tall cotton."

Joe grinned. "That's about the size of it."

"So what are you doing riding around in a patrol car, for heaven's sake?"

"I'm not the kind of man to sit around idle. I've got a lot of energy. When the mayor asked me to step in because the town was in a bind, my dad's arthritis hadn't flared yet and the two of us were in a bit of a tug-of-war out at the ranch."

"The two of you've done a lot of that—tugging at each other."

He shrugged. "Things are different now. Maybe it's maturity, or maybe it's because I've learned some things about my parents I hadn't known before."

She paused to look at him, not sure where he was going with the story.

"My dad pushed me when I was younger. Sports were his dream, and I always figured since it didn't work out for him, he was wanting to live his life through me. He's the one who wanted me to play ball, and he's the one who pushed me to go for a law degree. It seemed as if he wanted me to be somebody with a title, somebody he could brag about. I resented that."

"But that wasn't the case?"

He shook his head. "Like I said. I've since found out a few things I didn't know before. My dad had an opportunity to play pro football. Then my mom ran into complications in her pregnancy with me. My dad had to choose between training camp and taking care of mom. He chose my mom—us, really. He stayed in Darby to be a family man. He could have uprooted us to chase that dream, but he didn't. He stuck around and he stuck it out."

"That's very admirable."

"Yes, but I'd gotten it in my head that he regretted his decision and that's why he was always wanting so much more out of me. But it wasn't meanness, or trying to relive his life through me that caused him to push. It was just his way. He thought he was doing right by his boy by urging me to be the best."

"But his idea of what was best for you and yours were two different things?"

"Yeah. If I'd just taken the time to look at his and my mom's relationship, I'd have realized sooner that I didn't have to try so hard for approval. They've always had such a loving marriage. They made a home. That's what I'm looking to do, too."

She leaned a hip against the china hutch, abandoning the packing for the moment. "Make a home?"

"Yes. I thought it would work with Cindy, but it didn't."

"Cindy Granville from school, right?"

He nodded. "She wanted to be an attorney's wife. I wanted a family life in Darby."

"So where is she now?"

"Married to a partner in the firm I was working for in Austin."

And Joe was here, in Darby, searching for that family life. With her? Penny wondered. The intensity of his look seem to suggest it. But she'd misread his expressions and intentions before.

Besides, she wasn't the woman to give him the family he wanted.

She pushed her hair out of her face and sealed up the carton of china. "Will it be hard for your dad to give up running the ranch when you begin to devote your full time and attention to it?"

"That's the beauty of age and maturity, and perhaps inevitability, to a certain degree. My dad and I have become good friends. I'm looking forward to spending more time with him." He moved across the room, squatted down to take a box out of the dog's chewing range.

"Actually, Gramps left the ranch to me and the oil fields to Dad, so in essence, Dad's minding my inheritance for me. Truthfully, that's the main reason I accepted the position with the police department. With Dad and me on good terms, I wanted to ease into the ranch ownership, not just come in and start running a piece of land that my dad had lived and sweated on all of his life.''

''So why didn't your grandfather leave the land to your dad?''

''Because ranching was *my* dream.''

''And your sister?''

He lifted a photograph out of the box, studied it. ''Laura's in San Antonio. Happily married with a couple of kids. They come down for Sunday dinner about once a month.''

With her hands stuck in the back pockets of her shorts, she moved across the room to see what had snagged his attention in that box.

She went hot with embarrassment when she saw the photo he held. It was a picture of her as a child. Even at ten she looked serious and studious in her cat's-eye, plastic frame glasses. A real nerd. Although today, the glasses would probably be *en Vogue*.

She snatched the glossy from him. ''You don't want to see all this stuff.''

Instead of taking the hint, he lifted another photo from the box.

Penny sighed and knelt next to him, her head bent close to his as she studied the photograph. ''That's my mom and dad.''

Her parents made a handsome couple, Penny thought, still staring at the photograph. A young Errol Flynn and Grace Kelly. Too bad the images didn't reflect the truth.

''You've never talked about your mother.''

''I was brought up not to talk about her.''

His head whipped around, nearly butting hers. "Why?"

She tossed the picture back in the box and stood. She rarely trusted anyone with this secret. When she and her dad had come to live at Grandmother's, her mother was already gone. It was easy enough to lie—to make her mother seem like some ethereal angel who'd been brutally ripped from the world before her time. A story that was so far from the truth that it was pitiful.

Joe stood and watched the emotions flit across Penny's face. He needed to get back to work, but he had an idea he'd just opened a painful album of memories. He wanted to go to her, put his arms around her. Instead, he respected her unspoken need for distance.

"My mom was sick."

"Cancer?"

"Schizophrenia."

His brows shifted.

"She was on medication to control it, but she forgot to take it sometimes. I think that was on purpose, she didn't like taking the pills. She'd get paranoid, accuse the neighbors of trying to take me, bang on people's windows and peer into their houses. She would come up with the wildest stories, create scenes. People were always calling the cops on her."

"And you witnessed this as a child?"

"Yes."

"What about your father?"

"He had a hard time dealing with her. He tried his best to be tender with her, but sometimes he lost patience. He blew up one day, told her to take her damned pills. He left the house, and she grabbed me and left, too. It seemed like we just drove and drove, and she just kept repeating, 'take your pills, take your pills.''' Penny rubbed her forehead.

"We were at a motel. I fell asleep, but something woke me. My mother was rocking on the bed, repeating 'take your pills' over and over. It was dark. I couldn't see what she was doing. I just squeezed my eyes shut. The next morning, she was dead, the empty prescription bottle by her hand."

"Oh, man." Despite her shield, Joe breached it, moved right over to her and took her in his arms.

She rested her forehead against his chest. "I should have gotten up to see what she was doing, but I was afraid of her."

He rubbed her back. "I know. You were just a kid. You're not to blame."

She shrugged. "I know."

The shrug and the words were at odds with each other. She *did* blame herself. Joe held her for a bit longer. His reluctance to let her go was keen.

He felt bad that he hadn't known about Penny's mom. Penny had been a needy kid. She'd needed friendship and love, and he'd been insensitive to that. He'd slept with her, but had never asked her what made her glad or sad. He'd never asked about her family or even if she was happy.

He'd wanted her to help him pass a test. And then he'd wanted her body.

His list of things to atone for kept growing.

She pulled back from him, gathered her shield

around herself once more. He could almost see it happening, and it annoyed him.

"Okay," she said with a shaky laugh. "Enough personal war stories for one day. Get out of here and go to work, Chief. And ignore the aunts the next time they call. I'm a big girl and I can take care of myself."

He flicked a finger down her nose. "That wasn't the reason I came by. I always make it a point to introduce myself to anyone new in town."

"Well you fell down on the job big time today."

"How's that?"

"As I recall, you and Nathan nodded in passing, but didn't exchange a single friendly word."

His mouth kicked up at the corner. "So, okay. I was protecting my interests."

"I'm not anybody's interests, Colter."

"Oh, but you're mine. I'm *very* interested." He bent down, brushed his lips against hers.

She could have ducked away. Should have. But the kiss was over before she could decide whether her heart or her head would rule.

She licked her lips, looked up into hazel eyes that were shaded by the brim of his khaki Stetson.

"Catch you later, 007." He turned and walked out the door, leaving her standing there like a dumbstruck, lovesick teenager.

She shook her head, told herself to get a grip, yet still she watched him as he walked to the car, his stride confident, his shoulders broad.

Why did she have to be so drawn to that sexy smile and flirty personality?

An image of Rafe Alvarez flashed in her mind. She'd had a crush on the agent not all that long ago, but had realized soon enough that it was only a passing thing. They were best of friends—colleagues. And Rafe was happily married to Kendra Kincade—Kendra Alvarez now.

What Penny suddenly realized was the keen resemblance between Joe and Rafe. Dark hair and eyes, same build, same flirtatious ways. She nearly sighed.

Damn it, she'd been searching for Joe Colter in every man she'd met over the last sixteen years and hadn't realized it until just now.

Darned inconvenient. This wasn't her home anymore. For once she had a chance to be more than the nearly invisible woman in the background. She had the chance to exploit her sharp mind and conditioned body. She didn't have to take a back seat to anybody.

It was Joe's fault that she was feeling all this turmoil. She'd compared every man to him and obviously found them lacking.

That's why Joe Colter had been her first and *only* lover.

And that explained why her mind was playing tricks on her, making her entertain crazy thoughts of love after all this time.

Sixteen years of celibacy was bound to make any woman want to damn the consequences and go for broke.

BY ELEVEN O'CLOCK that night, Penny was exhausted. She'd sorted and packed all she intended to do for the day. Scout was busy making messes and trying to get his mouth around anything he could.

"Okay, boy. Let's go for a run and see if we can work off some of that excess energy." Yours *and* mine, she thought.

She changed into running clothes, retrieved the leash she'd bought along with all the other doggie paraphernalia, and clipped it to Scout's collar. Letting them both out the front door, she nearly tripped over the dog before they took each other's measure and worked out a choreographed step rhythm.

Most of the neighbors' lights were off, and since the closest streetlamp was clear down at the corner, it took a moment for her eyes to adjust to the dark. Although she couldn't see the clouds in the inky sky, she knew they were there, hiding the stars and making the air sticky with humidity. Thunder rumbled, and far off in the distance, lightning flashed.

Tongue lolling, Scout glanced up at her and they nearly ended up in a heap. "It's okay, boy. We've got a while yet before the storm hits."

They ran about three miles before turning back and heading for home. She was going to make darn sure this silly dog was worn out and would sleep rather than eat the furniture.

And hopefully her own body would be too tired to let her mind keep her awake with thoughts of Joe.

When they got back in the yard, Penny bent down to release the leash from Scout's collar.

"How was that, boy?" she asked, wiping sweat from her brow and pulling the spandex away from her breasts to try and stir some air. She could smell rain as the storm moved closer. The humidity was awful.

She saw the cat an instant before Scout did, but wasn't quick enough to get the leash snapped back in place. The dog took off like a shot.

Penny shook her head, deciding to let him go. Honestly. She ought to just let the darn dog walk himself. He was more puppy than dog. Perhaps that's why he was a stray. Someone didn't want to take the time to teach him not to eat shoes and run wild in the bushes. Puppies could pull stunts guaranteed to raise the blood pressure, but that was all part of growing. Scout simply needed some time and lessons.

She went up the front porch steps, put her hand on the screen door, then went absolutely still, the hairs on her arm standing on end.

Somebody was there.

Behind the screen door, the entry door was ajar. She knew she'd closed it to keep the cool air from escaping.

Her gun was inside the house. Great.

She glanced quickly over her shoulder to see if Georgia and Wanetta's lights were on. They weren't. So much for the neighborhood watch.

This time, she knew it wasn't Joe in her house. Granted, he'd surprised her before, but if he'd come back, his car would be at the curb.

The street was empty.

She started to quietly pull open the screen, turning back as she did so, but suddenly the light shining from the front room window winked off and the screen door swung outward with a force that knocked her back.

The wood frame caught her on the shoulder, cracked against her forehead. Before she could get her bearings, excruciating pain exploded in her head.

She opened her mouth to scream, but her world went black.

Chapter Six

Telling himself he was just being neighborly—and feeling like a damned teenager with a major crush—Joe found himself cruising down Penny's street.

Normally he didn't begrudge all the hours he put in, both at the department and on the ranch. But now that his mind was consumed with Penny Archer's return, and pursuing her, he was feeling the effects of overwork and stress.

It was close to midnight. Lightning split the heavens and thunder roared. Any minute now the sky would open up. He should have headed home hours ago, but someone had broken into the county hall of records and rifled through the archives located in the basement, forcing Joe to work overtime. The intruder had messed with several of the alphabetical files, but Joe couldn't tell what kind of information they'd been aiming for, or even if anything had been taken. That would require the clerks days of meticulous searching to narrow it down.

They'd only stumbled on the break-in after one of the patrolmen on duty had seen three youths running across the courthouse square. There were several groups of kids in Darby who were headed for delinquency if their parents didn't do something to curb it. Even small towns had their share of troubles.

But Joe had a nagging feeling this was more than kids pulling a prank. An itching at the back of his neck just wouldn't let him be.

One of his biggest worries right now was that Janelle's ex-husband, Don Gilard, was out of prison. There was a restraining order against him, but that rarely stopped a determined bully. Feeling uneasy, he'd driven by Janelle's place...and now he was in front of Penny's.

The house was dark, and he told himself it was for the best. She was like a drug in his system, and he really should give them both some space.

Thunder boomed and lightning lit the sky like a bright strobe.

He noticed the little collie on the porch.

Standing over a body.

He slammed on the brakes, rammed the truck's gearshift into Park and had the door open before the vehicle had even finished rocking.

As he ran up the walkway, several questions and impressions hit him at once. Had she fallen? Had someone attacked her?

The lights were off in the house and the front door was wide open. If someone had attacked her, ten to one they were long gone by now. Still, he unhooked the safety strap on his holstered gun as he dropped to his knees on the porch beside her.

His heart pounding hard enough to break a rib, he

checked for a pulse, found it strong and steady, and scooped her up against his chest.

PENNY FELT WARMTH surround her. And pain.

She struggled to lift her eyelids and nearly gave up when nausea swamped her.

"Come on, baby. That's it. Open your eyes."

Joe? She shifted—and moaned.

"Don't move. I've got you."

She opened her eyes all the way and found herself cradled in Joe's arms. The dog was whining and licking her face. A clap of thunder made her flinch. A bolt of lightning lit up the night, turning Joe's white shirt almost blue—with a dark smear of something slashed across the front.

She touched her fingers to the stain and they came away sticky. Blood?

"What in the world?"

"Just be still, would you?"

"Stop giving me orders." Her head hurt like a son of a gun and coherency was flooding back with the same intensity as the rain which had just begun to pour from a renegade cell in the sky.

"Somebody needs to give you orders," he said gently as he pressed a handkerchief to her temple. "Obviously you don't have sense enough not to get yourself half killed."

That stung. She knew it wasn't his intention, but still…her reputation was slipping. She was at a disadvantage lying here in his arms like this and she didn't like it. It made her feel vulnerable…and embarrassed.

"What happened?" he asked.

She shook her head and immediately realized that was a mistake. Some devil was having a field day inside her skull. "I took Scout for a run, and when I got back, I noticed the door was ajar. Before I could react, somebody rushed me."

"Did you get a look at him?"

"No. It happened too fast. I was looking at the dog, noticing that the neighbors' lights were out, and before I got fully turned back around I was blindsided by the door."

He transferred the blood-stained handkerchief to her hand, urged her to hold it and apply pressure to her wound, then propped her against the wall and drew his gun out of the holster. "You stay here."

"Joe—" She struggled to get to her feet, but he clamped a gentle yet firm hand on her shoulder.

"I mean it. You move and I swear I'll lock you up for obstruction of justice."

She rolled her eyes, found that the action hurt, and gave in. She was feeling woozy anyway. "I'm telling you, there's no one in the house, but go ahead. Knock yourself out."

Feeling like an idiot for letting someone get the jump on her this way, Penny rested her aching head back against the brick wall and wrapped her arm around Scout, burying her fingers in the collie's wet fur.

She was used to being the one people depended on—the agents in the Texas Confidential unit rarely made a move unless she knew about it and organized it. This role reversal felt odd. She'd come to think of herself as the capable one. Having someone—Joe especially—rescue her, unnerved her.

The lights winked on inside and Joe came back out.

"All clear," he said. "Although the place is a mess. I can't tell if you made it or someone else did."

"Maybe a little of both. I made some pretty good progress today sifting through stuff. But that progress resulted in quite a bit of disorganization." Her head was throbbing like mad and she didn't know if she wanted to move just yet. Nausea still flirted and nothing would embarrass her more than to get sick in front of Joe Colter.

Well, maybe getting knocked out in front of him, but that was already water under the bridge.

"Why do you keep showing up at my house like this?"

He took the handkerchief away from her forehead, daubed at the wound. "Damned if I know why since you're such a grouch, but I happen to like you."

Her lips twitched. "Look who's calling who a grouch."

"Yeah, well, it's a good thing I did show up. You'd have laid here and bled to death."

"Let's not get carried away—"

"Yes, let's." He scooped one arm beneath her knees and the other around her back and lifted her.

"Joe!"

"Hush." Shouldering open the door, he took her inside. "We're going to look at this cut on your head, then you're going to pack a bag and come out to the ranch with me."

She was so stunned by his bossiness—and him carrying her, that it was a moment before she could find her voice. Emotions were raging faster than she could process them.

No man had ever carried her in his arms. Her father hadn't been around much, and besides that, she simply wasn't the type of woman to inspire such behavior.

"I'm not spending the night with you."

"More than a night if I have any say about it." He set her on the closed lid of the commode in the bathroom and examined her forehead.

"You don't have any say about it," she said. "I'm in the middle of a project here, and I can't very well do that from your ranch, now can I?"

"Then I'll move in here."

"Don't be ridiculous." Her heart vaulted into her throat and did a little jig. Some wild part of her wanted to say yes, yes, yes. But that would lead to more than either one of them could handle. She couldn't allow herself to get involved with Joe Colter. She was leaving in a few weeks. Nothing good could come of a relationship between them.

And that's what would happen if they were under the same roof. Her willpower simply wouldn't stand up to the temptation.

"You'll have a heck of a bruise and be sore, but I don't think you'll need stitches. Hold on, this'll sting." He pressed a cotton ball soaked with peroxide to her head.

"Ouch, damn it!" She shoved at his hand. "That hurts."

"I warned you. Now, don't be a baby."

She glared at him. "You're not staying here."

"Then come home with me."

"I can take care of myself."

He paused, gave her biceps a gentle squeeze, then turned his attention back to her wound. "This goose egg on your noggin begs to differ."

"Oh, for Pete's sake. Can you stand there and tell me nobody's ever gotten the jump on you?"

"Be silly to try since it was you who did it."

"There you go, then. If I can take you, I can certainly hold my own if something like this happens again. Besides, I'll be on guard now."

"You're missing the point, Pen. Have you been gone so long that you've forgotten the closeness of small towns? The willingness of neighbors and friends to watch out for each other?"

"Watching out for and smothering are two different things."

"I wonder why you're protesting so." He put a bandage over the cut, watched her with an intensity that caused her to squirm. Then very deliberately, he leaned down and pressed a kiss to the wound. "Could it be you don't trust yourself to sleep in the same house with me without jumping my bones?"

Her pulse leaping from that impromptu kiss, she sputtered. "Get real."

"Okay, tough girl. You're immune to me." He found a bottle of aspirin in the medicine chest, shook out a couple and handed them to her along with a glass of water. "So, which will it be? My couch or yours?"

She swallowed the pills. "Neither."

"Wrong answer. Of course there's always another alternative."

"And that is?"

"I could lock you up."

She laughed in his face. "I'd like to see you try it."

"Careful who you dare, little girl. I'm tired and hungry and more upset than I want to admit over seeing you laid out on the porch. I'm likely to lose my temper."

She shook her head, felt the bandage tug. Despite his high-handed manner, his concern was touching. "You're being awfully stubborn."

"Just listen to the pot call the kettle black. Look, you're in my town. That makes you my responsibility. It's my duty to protect you." He held up his hand when she would have argued. "Too many strange things have been going on these last couple of days for my peace of mind. Until I get to the bottom of it, let me watch your back. Partners. You can relate to that, can't you? I'm sure you deal with partners as backup."

She shrugged, not really answering. He did look tired. "What other things are happening?"

He raked a hand through his hair, shook his head. "First things first. My couch or yours?"

"Mine, damn it!" Although she had every right to be exasperated, she shouldn't have raised her voice. It set off the evil men inside her head. She moaned, started to rub her temples and encountered the bandage instead.

Tears filled her eyes, mortifying her beyond words.

"Shh, baby, don't do that. Come on, now." He had her in his arms before she could blink the moisture away. Wanting to be tough, unable to fight the emotions, she rested her cheek against his broad chest and let him have the lead. She was too done in to do anything else.

He took her into the front room, sat with her on the couch. "I ought to take you over to the clinic and have that cut looked at."

She sniffed. "It's fine. I'll put ice on it."

"Right. Ice. I'll get it." He eased her onto the cushions. "Can I trust you not to do the cha-cha around the living room while I'm gone?"

She gave a watery laugh. "I think we're fairly safe on that score."

He smiled softly, trailed his fingers lightly, quickly over her cheek. "I should call this in, have somebody come over and see if they can lift any prints."

"Not tonight, Joe. At a glance, it doesn't look like anything's missing. And I'm just not up to dealing with the mess of fingerprint dust on top of everything else."

He gazed down at her for a long moment, then nodded and went into the kitchen, returning several minutes later with ice cubes wrapped in a dishtowel.

He sat down, positioned a pillow in his lap and urged her to lay back. Gently, he pressed the cold compress to her head, using his thumb to wipe away the moisture from beneath her eyes.

"Thank you. I don't know why I'm acting like such a baby. I guess I'm just tired."

"Tough night. Try to stay awake for a while, okay? You've probably got a slight concussion."

"You really should go home, Joe."

"Hush. We've already been over this. This'll be much easier on both of us. I'm wearing myself out chasing after you."

She smiled. "Nobody asked you to chase after me."

"Turns out I can't seem to help myself."

That statement made her giddy, but she darn sure didn't want to go there. "So tell me about these strange goings-on that you mentioned."

"Someone broke into the county records department tonight."

"Could you tell what they were looking for?"

"No. The only thing disturbed were the files in the basement. Rochelle, who's in charge of records isn't sure if files that old were put into the computer."

"How long has Rochelle been working in records?"

"A couple of years, I guess. I'm not sure."

"Seems weird that somebody rifled the hall of records the same night someone was in my house. I can't imagine a connection, but I do have a suspicious mind."

Joe stroked her hair absently. "More common ground between us."

Her gaze lifted to his. "Stay on task, Joe."

He grinned. "Right."

"Did my grandmother have enemies that you knew of?"

"No. Do you?"

"What?"

"Have enemies."

She stiffened. "Meaning that since I came back to town strange things are happening?" She wondered if she should mention the hang up calls and clicking noises over the phone lines. Miffed a bit at his inference, she kept silent. Who would have thought a simple trip to her hometown to deal with her grandmother's estate would be riddled with such drama?

"I'm just trying to cover the bases, babe. If someone's gunning for you, I'd like to know about it."

"Nobody's after me. The last case I worked on is all wrapped up and tied with a pretty bow. I didn't make a single enemy."

"And that case was?"

She knew he expected her to sidestep. She surprised him by answering. "The Calderone-Rialto drug cartel."

Joe whistled. "I saw that bust on the national news. The Feds had been trying to bring down that group for years."

She smiled, feeling sleepy. Thankfully, the aspirin were taking the edge off her pain. "They finally wised up and called in the experts."

"And no loose ends, you say?"

"We don't leave loose ends. So let's try a different avenue here." It was her gentle way of closing the subject of her job. And Joe allowed it, even though it was clear that something was still making him nervous.

"I've got another nagging thought," he said, "but chances are I'm just being jumpy."

"What's the thought?"

"Don Gilard."

"Janelle's ex? Do you really think he's going to show up?"

"Yes. He hurt Janelle pretty bad and she testified against him. I didn't trust the guy in school, and I sure as hell don't trust him now. Thing is, I can't figure out why Gilard would be rifling through old city files."

"Looking for marriage records?" Penny asked.

"Janelle and Jim were only married a couple of years ago. I don't think those records would be in the basement."

"Don wouldn't know that."

He gazed at her thoughtfully. "We're probably grabbing at straws."

"Probably. Why don't you contact his parole officer, make sure he's checking in regularly." Penny decided she'd call Mitchell, see if there was a locator available who'd be willing to do some unofficial moonlighting. A good agent could pinpoint Gilard's whereabouts, get close to him and find out his intentions. And the locators Mitchell used, ex-agents who still liked to keep their hand in the game—were some of the best.

"Yeah, I'll do that." He stroked her forehead, keeping his fingers clear of her wound. The rhythmic movement and the gentle tap of the rain on the roof lulled Penny and she couldn't keep her eyes open any longer.

WHEN PENNY WOKE UP the next morning, she was in her bed and the rich fragrance of coffee filled the house.

Joe was still here.

She touched her forehead, winced. Well, this was going to be damned inconvenient. Just bending over to brush her teeth had the blood pooling and pounding at her temple, making the wound feel the size of a football.

She took out her contact lenses to clean them, considered not putting them back in. The sound of Joe in her kitchen—talking to somebody, she realized now—made up her mind. She popped the discs back in and went through ten extra minutes of wrestling with pots of shadow, lip gloss and a mascara wand.

She removed the bandage, deciding the wound was less conspicuous that way. Since she didn't wear bangs, she couldn't cover up the bump on her head, but she pulled her hair forward anyway. Honestly. Now she looked like a bad imitation of an old movie actress.

Disgusted with her uncharacteristic vanity, she left the bathroom, lured by the smell of coffee. A shot of caffeine with a bottle of aspirin via an open vein was her first choice. Barring that, she went directly past Wanetta and Georgia—whose mouths dropped open at the sight of her—and elbowed Joe aside to reach for a cup.

"Good morning, sunshine," Joe commented with a grin.

She burned her mouth and nearly spilled the dark brew down the small bit of cleavage showing past her scoop-neck top. "Morning," she mumbled.

"Let me help you with that." He started to daub her chest with a dishtowel.

Penny glared at him and stepped back.

"My land," Georgia exclaimed. "Don't tease the girl, Joe. Sister, come look at this horrible injury," she said to Wanetta.

It was very difficult for Penny to stand still under Georgia and Wanetta's clucking and Joe's sexy grin. She felt about as friendly as a riled up hornet.

"We saw Joe's truck—not that we were being nosy about your overnight houseguests—"

"He slept on the couch," Penny said quickly. *I think.* She looked at Joe. He still had that enigmatic smile on his face. Doggone it, he knew she was in a crummy mood and he actually thought it was funny.

"Of course he did, dear. And he told us all about your troubles. Why, I'm just sick that Wanetta and I went to bed early. Our television program was a rerun and to tell the truth, we just got bored. It's age, I think. But we'll not do that again. Why, sister and I will stand watch, take turns—"

"Georgia," Penny said gently. She set down her coffee cup and took a hand of each of her neighbors in hers. "I'm fine. It's just a little bump on the head and there's nothing you could have done to prevent it."

"Who would do such a thing?" Wanetta asked.

"Probably kids thinking the house was empty and an easy mark." She glanced out the window when she heard a vehicle pull into the driveway. The sign on the door panel of the service truck said William's Glass.

Penny raised a brow at Joe.

"They're here to replace that window. That's how the perp got in."

"Oh," Penny said, her brain still not functioning at full speed. "I assumed whoever it was came in the front door."

"You left it open?"

"If you recall I was out running. My clothes were a little light on pockets."

"Woman, in your line of work, I'd think security would be first and foremost on your mind."

"Not in Darby." She shrugged. "Despite what you think, I'm not that jaded."

"Well, work on getting that way, would you? I don't want to come here and find your doors unlocked again."

"Penny has a point, Joe. It's been many a year since we've felt the need to lock our doors if we're just going out for a walk."

"When's the last time you and Wanetta went walking at eleven o'clock at night?"

Georgia looked at Penny. "You couldn't sleep, dear?"

Penny's gaze met Joe's. Of course she couldn't sleep. A certain outlaw cowboy had kissed her, called her 007, and left her standing in her front room with her mouth agog and her hormones in a panic. She'd still be twisted in knots at eleven o'clock that night.

"I run to keep in shape," she said to the aunts.

"Oh. Well, then. I hear exercise is good for relaxation. Supposed to be good for the sex life, too, although that's a bit off the subject."

Way off the subject, Penny thought, nearly choking on a swallow of coffee.

"But Joe does have a point," Georgia continued. "It will behoove us all to be a bit more cautious. Can't have strangers coming in and knocking us over the head. You've a gun, don't you dear?"

"Of course she has a gun," Wanetta answered for Penny. "Who do you think you're talking to?"

Georgia whipped around and glared at Wanetta. "You've just heard her say she feels perfectly safe in Darby. Perhaps—"

"I do feel safe," Penny interrupted before things could get out of hand. "And I do have a gun, but—"

"Just to be on the safe side, she's coming out to the ranch with me," Joe said.

Penny opened her mouth to refute that arrogant assumption, but the aunts jumped in like ducks on a june bug, deciding that was the best solution under the circumstances.

While everyone else in the kitchen was discussing how best for her to run her life and where she should sleep, Penny went to let the workmen in to fix the glass. Since they were all talking about her as though she wasn't even there, she figured it'd be a while yet before they noticed her missing.

Her head was starting to hurt again.

Joe FOUND HER in the bedroom sitting in the middle of the bed sorting through a jewelry box.

She looked up. "Are they gone?"

"Yes."

"I'm sorry for being so rude. I just wasn't up to so much…conversation first thing this morning."

Joe grinned. "Understandable." He came into the room. "So, how's the head?"

"Sore."

"Figured. Did you get a chance to have a look around for anything missing?"

"Yes. My wallet was open. About forty dollars was taken. Good thing I don't keep all my cash in the same place. Still, my guess is it was kids looking for beer money. Maybe even those delinquents you mentioned."

"You could be right, but I'm not willing to pass this off quite that easily." He glanced around the room. "Did you want to pack an overnight bag?"

The switch in subjects had her scrambling to catch up. "No."

"I'll rephrase. Pack an overnight bag, Penny."

"Here's a tip for you, Chief. I don't take orders nicely."

"So, fine. Take them not nicely."

"Joe…"

He sat down on the bed, put a finger over her lips, then shifted her hair and examined her injury. "You're so stubborn and independent," he said softly. "You were as a kid, too. Come home with me, Pen."

"Joe—"

"Just spend the day with me. I'm off today. I'll worry if you're here in town and I'm out at the ranch. Just come hang out with me. Partners spending a friendly day together."

Oh, he didn't play fair. Truthfully, her head was sore and she didn't feel up to trying to pack today.

Not knowing he'd already won the argument, Joe said, "If you want to prove how tough you are, take a ride with me. I'll put you on a horse and you can abuse your head that way."

She laughed at the absurdity of his suggestion. But she really wanted to spend the day with Joe. It was so tough to decide what to keep and what to give away of her grandmother's stuff—and it was sad that there was nobody to divide it with.

"Okay, I'll come to the ranch with you. But I'll have your sworn promise that you'll bring me back home tonight."

He gave her a cocky grin. "Hey, if you can't trust your partner, who can you trust?"

"You're pushing it, Chief."

Chapter Seven

The land around Darby was so different from the desert terrain surrounding the Smoking Barrel ranch in west Texas.

Here, thanks to a particularly rainy season, the vast prairies and knolls were lush and green. Vibrant bluebonnets and Indian Paintbrush grew along the roadside and across the land.

And Joe's ranch was as beautiful as Penny remembered. Beneath an archway proclaiming the Circle C, a ribbon of blacktop led visitors onto the Colter property. Pecans and oaks lined the drive like stately sentinels guarding secrets and gossip, yet welcoming with open branches as though inviting the world to come on over for a barbecue or a swim.

The driveway came to dead end at a *T* where a small pecan orchard lay straight ahead. Joe turned to the left when Penny had expected him to go right—toward his parents' house. They traveled along this different fork in the road for perhaps another quarter of a mile as Penny absorbed the magnitude of his obviously prosperous cattle ranch.

"You changed addresses." The sight that lay ahead of her was so grand she could hardly take it in.

"Gramps left me the main house. Cindy wouldn't have been keen on living with my folks anyway."

"She was an idiot if she wasn't keen on living in *this* place," Penny said as they pulled up in front of the main house.

It was white, two stories, with dormers, balconies, columns and porches. An eclectic mix of architecture that made it absolutely grand rather than gaudy. She hadn't even known the house was here, hidden this way by the pecan trees.

"Then I guess she was an idiot," Joe said with a grin.

Penny glanced at him. "Sorry. I didn't mean to speak badly of her."

"That's okay. She's much happier living in the city."

Penny got out of the truck and breathed in air fresh from last night's summer rain mixed with the familiar smell of animals. A carpet of green sod and beds of flowers and shrubs surrounded the house. Longhorn cattle grazed in the distance as did horses, while a half dozen ranch hands went about their work in corrals and barns.

"I can see why you want to devote your time here. This is quite a legacy your grandfather left you."

"Yep. Now it'd be nice to fill this big old house with kids to carry on that legacy."

He said it so easily. That's how one usually spoke of a dream they were confident would one day come to pass.

Pain flooded her, and it had nothing to do with the bump on her head. Someday Joe *would* fill this house with babies and laughter and love.

And she wouldn't be the lucky woman to share that joy with him.

"Hey, you okay?" He came around the truck and tipped up her chin, searching her eyes. "Head hurting?"

"A little." It wasn't a lie. "I'm okay, though."

"Tough girl."

"Yeah, that's me."

A fairly new pickup pulled in behind Joe's truck. Penny shaded her eyes and watched as Joe's parents got out and came toward them.

"I figured they'd be right behind us," he said. "I don't often bring home a woman, so I imagine my mom's practically salivating to check out the situation. She lives in hope that I'll settle down."

Penny was pleased to know that Joe didn't bring women out here, yet dismayed that she was about to become the center of attention. Especially looking like she'd been in a brawl.

"How'd they know you brought a woman?"

Joe gave her a sheepish look. "Mom's not the only one who wants to see me settled again. I imagine one of the guys called the house." He tipped his head toward the barn where several men milled about, trying not to be too obvious.

Penny flicked her hair behind her ear, felt her nerves hum beneath her skin. She'd never been overly shy, and she wasn't going to start acting that way now.

Cyrus Colter was still quite handsome, she noticed. A big man with wide shoulders and a full head of snow-white hair even though he was only in his late fifties. And Donna Colter was as petite and pretty and serene-looking as Penny remembered.

"Penny Archer," Donna exclaimed and drew Penny into a hug. "It's been so long. And I hear you've got quite the prestigious job—oh, my word, what happened to your poor head. Joe?" She looked at her son as though it was his responsibility to answer for such a horrible injury.

Penny felt acutely embarrassed. Everybody thought she was an exciting, capable government agent, and this conspicuous lump on the head was like a great big badge of ineptness. Sporting it, she was starting to wish she was just plain old Penny.

"It's nice to see you, Mrs. Colter."

"Oh, fiddle. Call me, Donna. Do tell me what happened, honey."

"I ran into a door as someone was coming out."

"A break-in at her grandmother's," Joe clarified.

Penny gave him a thank-you-very-much look, to which he grinned.

"Oh, no." Donna clucked some more, not turning her loose, even though it was clear that Cyrus was waiting his turn to greet their guest. "Crime in Darby. That's practically unheard of. And I'm so sorry about your grandmother's passing."

"Thank you, Mrs...Donna." She turned and held out her hand to Joe's father.

"It's Cyrus," he said, accepting her hand before she could address him formally.

Penny nodded. Respect and curiosity, it was there in their faces—with a heavy emphasis on curiosity. "You're looking well, Cyrus."

He laughed, that booming, backslapping laugh she remembered so well. "Need some glasses, sweet pea?"

"Cyrus!" Donna elbowed her husband in the ribs, scandalized.

Penny chuckled, knowing he wasn't insulting her, but alluding to his own limping gait and swollen knuckles, a result of the ravages of rheumatoid arthritis.

"Nope," she said. "Got 'em right here on my eyeballs."

Cyrus stepped closer, peered at her wound, and then into her brown eyes where softly colored discs floated over her irises. "Good thing I don't have to wear those things. I'd forever be picking dust out of them."

"You want to quit staring into my houseguest's eyes, Dad?" Joe said.

Cyrus laughed again, loud and long. "Territorial son of a gun. Houseguest, huh?"

"Visitor," Penny corrected.

"We're negotiating," Joe added.

"I believe I received a sworn promise," she said, turning a pointed gaze on Joe.

"Did you?" he asked softly, meeting her gaze and holding it as though they were the only two people present. It was an intimate look that should not have been displayed in public.

And come to think of it, he hadn't actually given his word. He'd sidestepped.

"Well," Donna cut in smoothly. "When you decide, the two of you come on over to the house for dinner. Laura and the girls will be here this afternoon. I'm sure she'd love to see you, Penny. Come on, Cyrus. Let's leave the kids be."

Penny rubbed her sweaty palms on her hips. She knew she looked just fine in her jeans, boots and snug T-shirt, but an attack of nerves zinged her. Laura had been two years ahead of her in high school and had hardly known Penny existed. Not because Laura was a snob. They just didn't run in the same circles. The couple of times Penny had been out to the ranch to tutor Joe, Laura had been out on a date or off somewhere else.

Given the Colters were virtual strangers, it felt odd now to be welcomed by the family with open arms.

And what in the world was she thinking like this for anyway? It had been a long time since she'd felt uncomfortable or out of place in a social situation.

Why was it that Joe Colter and anything associated with him pushed her buttons?

She turned back to Joe. "You did that on purpose."

"Did what?"

"Gave the impression that there was something intimate going on between us."

"Oh, but there is."

Her heart nearly pounded out of her chest. And with the swift rush of adrenaline came a debilitating throb at her temple. She swayed and his hands were right there to steady her, his intense eyes not missing a thing.

"Let's get you inside where it's cool."

For once she was going to give in gracefully. "I'm not your houseguest."

"That's fine, 007. I'll just be yours."

FROM ACROSS the room, Joe watched Penny laughing and talking with his sister as though they'd known each other for years. His nieces, Megan and Trudy, hung on every word, clearly in awe of her, and Penny made it a point to include them as though they were adults instead of ten- and seven-year-olds.

Joe felt odd emotions knocking beneath his breast-bone. Her poise and her ability to put others at ease were a gift. It was as though she was the hostess and they were the welcome guests. She was an attentive listener, gracious and quick to laugh.

It was a gift he didn't think she was even aware she possessed.

Just watching her was pure pleasure, the way she moved, the way she spoke, a gentle hand on the arm here, a quick smile there. Smart, efficient, sexy. Admiration swelled inside him. Within minutes, she'd blended in like one of the family—something his ex-wife hadn't been able to accomplish in eight years.

And that's when Joe realized he'd been waiting all his life for someone like Penny. Exactly like Penny. For forever, it seemed. He'd made mistakes along the way, and he had to wonder if this was why he hadn't fought harder to hang on to his marriage.

Every time his gaze rested on Penny's smooth-as-silk skin and athletic body, he couldn't help but flash on that single, fantasy-inspiring weekend they'd spent together. After all this time, he hadn't been able to get it out of his mind.

He hadn't been able to get Penny Archer out of his mind.

He wanted her like mad.

Full of contrasts and contradictions, she appeared so aloof, but there was a fire that burned beneath that exterior. A fire he wanted to touch again and again.

One he had every intention of stoking.

As though she could feel his simmering thoughts, her gaze lifted, touched on his, then slammed back and held with the same heat. She knew exactly what he was thinking. He could see it there in her eyes and he went from zip to hard in an instant.

"Dinner," Donna called, jolting him. He pulled his gaze away before he ended up embarrassing them both.

"I get to sit by Penny," Megan sang.

"No, I do," Trudy argued.

"Girls," Laura admonished. "No fighting."

"There are two sides to me," Penny said gently.

"But Uncle Joe will want one of them," Trudy complained, somehow knowing she'd end up losing out to her older sister.

Penny looked up at him, smiled slowly, held his gaze long enough to turn him to putty. "Well, Uncle Joe can't always have everything he wants, now can he?"

There was a provocative taunt to her words and Joe felt the blood rush right back to his groin.

Cyrus came up behind him, slapped him on the back, then went to take his place at the table. "Ha! Girl's full of sass but with those muscles I'd advise you not to tangle with her."

When Penny started to move past, Joe said softly, "What do you think, 007? You in the mood to tangle?"

She paused, looked him square in the eye, a smile playing at the corners of her full lips. "Are you in the mood to lose?"

Joe laughed out loud and stepped aside as she herded both little girls into chairs on either side of hers.

Yes, by damn, they would tangle. And he couldn't wait.

IT WAS DARK when they got back to Penny's house. And though she hadn't been able to stop him from coming in, she'd told him to leave his duffel bag in the truck.

"You're not spending the night," she said when he'd searched all the rooms. "I don't need a baby-sitter. I'm perfectly capable of taking care of myself."

"So you say." He linked their hands together and tugged her down on the couch.

"Joe!" What had gotten into him? Ever since that exchange before dinner, he'd been like a cat watching a baby bird, waiting to make his move. Penny wasn't sure she liked feeling like a baby bird.

"So, tell me Miss Tough Girl, how come some smart agent hasn't snapped you up before now?"

She laughed, started to relax. "I'm not interested

in being snapped up. Especially by an agent. They're pretty much a 'no commitment' bunch.'' Although four of them had gotten married recently, which blew that theory all to Hades.

"No serious relationships, then?"

"I was dating a gentleman a while ago. A friend fixed us up, but we mutually, amicably dumped each other a few weeks back."

"Why?"

She shrugged. "No spark, I guess. We both led busy lives, and neither of us seemed to care enough to make time for each other."

"Just as well," he murmured, and brushed the hair away from her cheek. "I'd hate to have to run off my competition."

Before she even registered his intent, he tipped up her chin and lowered his lips to hers.

Stunned, she jerked back as though she'd been zapped by a jolt of electricity.

Quietly, steadily, he held her gaze. A fire burned in his hazel eyes. So did purpose.

He was going kiss her. And she was going to let him, regardless of the consequences.

Because she wanted to kiss Joe Colter. Wanted it more than air to breathe.

He hooked his hand around the back of her neck, drew her to him, still holding her gaze…a gaze that gave him permission.

This time when his mouth touched hers, she was ready.

He was an absolute expert at this, she thought numbly. He didn't try to attack or devour, didn't rush to get to the main goal. Without opening his mouth, he took his time, nipped and tasted, seduced and aroused. She smelled the clean scent of soap on his hands as he framed her face and angled her head for better access.

She moaned, leaned into the kiss and opened her mouth when he at last sought entrance. Sensations poured over her, so new and yet so familiar. Coherency scattered to the wind as she pressed against him, stunned and pleased and floating on a haze of desire.

His hand dropped to her neck, her collarbone, to the hem of her T-shirt and beneath. When his palm cupped her breast, she jolted.

She wasn't a virgin. But neither was she experienced. The shock of intimacy after so very long brought her crashing back to reality.

He eased back, studied her.

"This wasn't on the agenda," she whispered, unable to look away.

"Oh, yes it was. It has been for sixteen years." He pressed his lips against the wound at her temple. "But since you're operating under a handicap, I can wait a while longer."

His ego astonished her. It shouldn't have, but it did. Not wanting him to see just how much his words aroused her, she smacked him with a throw pillow. "Awfully sure of yourself, aren't you?"

"Yes."

A smile tugged at her mouth. Joe had always been stimulating company. He kept her on her toes. Never mind what he did to her hormones. "Get out of here, Colter."

He raised a brow. "Who said I was leaving?"

"I did. And don't give me that I'm-the-chief look. I'm more than a match for you."

He took his time deciding if he would give in or put up a fight. Finally, he stood and walked to the front door she was now holding open. "You're only throwing me out because I'm letting you."

The challenge was nearly irresistible. "Don't be so sure. You haven't seen all my moves."

"Oh, but I will." He caught her chin in his hand, bent down to cover her smiling lips with his, lingered for a long moment. It was a kiss filled with male assurance and promise. A thrilling promise. "I definitely will."

Penny watched him put his hat on his head and go down the front walk, his shoulders back, his gaze alert as he scanned the darkness.

Slowly, she closed the door, twisted the lock, leaned the uninjured side of her forehead against the wood, and noted that she was trembling.

She was headed for trouble. Big trouble. And she couldn't seem to find the gumption to change course.

She was going to have to work on that. Diligently.

"GOT A MINUTE, JOE?"

Joe looked up from the paperwork on his desk. The mayor stood in his office doorway—if it could even be called an office. Four walls and a door, it was about the size of a closet.

"Come on in, Ben. Have a seat."

Ben Upton pushed away from the doorway and

lowered his bulky frame into a chair in front of Joe's desk.

"How's it going, son?"

"Busy."

"So I'd heard. Any leads on the break-in over at the records hall?" he asked, placing his hat in his lap.

Joe shook his head. "Rochelle's still working on the files to see what's missing, but no luck so far. The boys weren't able to lift any good prints."

"So, no idea what they were after?"

"Not yet."

"Heard someone rifled through Agnes Archer's house, too. Any connection there?"

Something in the mayor's tone set Joe on edge. "Not that we know of. Probably kids looking for easy cash."

"The granddaughter's some kind of undercover agent, isn't she?"

"Something like that." Joe put down his pen. "What's on your mind, Ben?"

"Seems odd that since she showed up, crime's come to Darby."

"We've had our share of crime." He kept his voice even, but it was an effort.

The mayor shrugged. "All I'm sayin' is folks are askin' questions. They're starting to worry if it's safe to take the dogs out for a walk."

And this being an election year, the mayor felt the need to flex his muscles a bit.

"I'm a little surprised at what you seem to be suggesting," Joe said, his tone tight. "Penny Archer is a citizen of Darby, too. This is her hometown. Yet I don't hear you asking after her welfare and safety.''

At Joe's annoyed tone, Ben quickly backtracked and came down off his high horse. ''You're right, of course. I'm out of line.'' He laughed and fingered the brim of his hat. ''You know me. Not enough going on to keep me busy and when something does happen I get overly excited. I've got a bad habit of letting my alligator mouth overload my you-know-what.'' He stood. ''I'll get out of your hair. Keep me posted.''

THE GRAND OPENING of Kelly's Book Nook was off to an excellent start. People were browsing and buying and enjoying refreshments.

Penny had almost talked herself out of coming, feeling conspicuous with this nasty bruise and healing cut on her head.

But rather than a badge of ineptness as she'd come to view the wound, her friends thought it added to her mystique. They flocked around her like a bunch of ghouls.

''Wow,'' Kelly said. ''That's a beaut. Does it hurt?''

Penny rolled her eyes. ''What do you think, Kel?''

''Sorry. Imagine somebody breaking in like that.''

''Oh, but you're probably used to this rough-and-tumble stuff aren't you?'' Pam asked. ''I imagine a knock on the head is nothing compared to people blowing up stuff in front of you and getting hit by flying debris.''

Penny sputtered out a laugh. ''Where in the world did you get that kind of an imagination? You've either been spending too much time in the adventure fiction section of this bookstore or you should be writing a book yourself.''

''I just might do that,'' Pam said. ''Let me interview you and I'll write a splashy, action packed tell-all that'll make us both famous.''

''Damn,'' Kelly said, looking toward the front of the store. Penny's hand automatically went to the purse hanging at her side, then relaxed when she saw who'd just come in the door.

''I though we were going to skate by without running into good old Lanie Dubois. Did you see the way she just turned her nose up at the fruit-and-cheese tray?''

''Naturally,'' Pam said. ''It's not caviar like *daddy* serves.''

''Be nice,'' Janelle said. ''She's coming this way.''

''Well, hey, Kelly. Isn't this just the cutest little store,'' Lanie said in a voice that dripped sugar.

Cute? Penny thought, glancing around. It was a lot more than cute. The bookstore occupied about twelve hundred square feet with wide aisles that held thousands of meticulously shelved books from self-help to romance, both new and used.

Kelly plastered a smile on her face even though she clearly knew she was being patronized. ''It was nice of you to come, Lanie. We're always happy to welcome new customers. Feel free to browse, have something to eat.''

''Oh, I didn't come to browse— I'm much too busy to read. And I'm watching my figure.'' She ran her hands over her short yellow skirt and tugged at her matching blazer. "I just stopped by to check out our investment. Since it appears you're up to your eyeballs in debt to us, that makes us sort of like partners, wouldn't you say?"

Penny wanted to pull out Lanie's red-from-a-bottle hair. Kelly was nervous enough about taking on such a huge venture. This was supposed to be a celebration, and Lanie was deliberately trying to ruin it.

Lanie Dubois had always thought she was above everyone else. And that hit a nerve.

"Not partners," Penny interrupted ever so politely. "The way I understand it, Kelly is a sole proprietor, an entrepreneur. And you're an employee of the financial institution that had the good business sense to recognize and endorse a viable, potentially profitable establishment."

Lanie frowned and looked at Penny, clearly not liking being referred to as a mere employee. Everyone knew her daddy was the bank president.

Her penciled brows rose as though she were a queen looking down on a lowly subject. "I'm sorry, I'm having trouble recalling your name."

Kelly and Pam cut their gazes to Penny. She gave an inward sigh. The silent plea for action was there, and Penny felt honor-bound to pick up the ball.

In school they'd been a group. Penny was the brain, Kelly was the outgoing one—though not the cheerleader type, she was everyone's friend. Janelle was the sweet one, a pleaser. And Pam was the class clown with a love of animals, dragging home every stray in the neighborhood. They hadn't been popular girls, but they'd been a foursome, they'd stuck together.

The brain, the friendly one, the sweet one and the clown.

And they'd raised plenty of hell.

"Penny Archer," she said, knowing full well Lanie knew her name but was being difficult. Under the guise of holding out her hand in introduction, she deliberately caught her fingers on the latch of her purse. Designed with a special, quick access compartment, the leather fell open to reveal her gun. "Oops."

Lanie's eyes widened, and she gasped. "Oh, my goodness. I'd heard you were an agent or something. You don't actually *shoot* people, do you?"

Penny dropped her hand, and took her time closing her purse.

She hooked the latch, looked directly at Lanie. "Yes. I do...but only when they make me mad."

Kelly and Pam covered their mouths, their eyes wide and filled with mirth.

Janelle's jaw dropped.

Russ, who'd just walked up behind his wife, raised a brow.

Penny simply stood there innocently fingering the now closed latch on her purse, staring at Lanie with bored eyes until the other woman whirled around and walked away.

"Thank you," Kelly said softly after Lanie left.

"Don't mention it," Penny said. "Always happy to help out a pal." It was a silly stunt she'd pulled— even though her friends had asked her to do that very thing just days ago in Kelly's kitchen. But she couldn't just stand by and watch some catty rich girl put down her friend.

"Did I miss something here?" Russ asked, a smile pulling at his lips. His gaze, when it touched on his wife, was filled with loving indulgence.

"We were just enacting a fantasy," Pam said to her husband. She smacked a kiss to his cheek, then hooked one arm through Penny's and managed to get the other around both Kelly and Janelle. "Come on, girls, let's go ruin our figures. Except for Miss Muscles here. A fat cell wouldn't be caught dead or alive on that body."

"Get out," Penny teased. God, this felt good. She hadn't realized how much she'd missed having girl-friends to act crazy with. She'd been living in a pre-dominately man's world, isolated on the Smoking Barrel ranch with a bunch of male agents and cow-boys. She hadn't felt the lack of female companion-ship and camaraderie until she'd come home to Darby.

Home to Darby. The thought made her feel both warmth and sadness.

Chapter Eight

The thing about a nice car was that you rarely had to worry about it malfunctioning. That's why Penny nearly went into a panic when the Cadillac started jerking and lurching and finally quit on her no more than ten minutes after she'd left the bookstore.

Fighting the sudden lack of power steering, she muscled the coasting car to the edge of the road, scaring an armadillo back into the bushes. At least she'd saved the ugly creature from becoming roadkill.

This is ridiculous! she thought. Was this town a jinx or something? It seemed she went from one calamity to the next.

Pulling the release, she got out, lifted the hood, and peered into the engine compartment, thoroughly bewildered. She nearly snorted in disgust. Like she'd even know what to do under here. Cars nowadays operated on a bunch of computer chips. Even if the darn thing spoke to her and told her what was wrong, she wouldn't have a clue how to fix it.

She heard the crunch of gravel beneath tires and peered around the edge of the hood.

Joe Colter, grinning behind the wheel of his squad car came to a stop inches from her back bumper.

She sighed. Wouldn't you just know it.

Was she doomed to forever look inept in front of this man?

Hat on his head, hips loose, he ambled toward her.

"Are you following me?" she asked, not bothering to keep the annoyance out of her tone.

"Maybe." His appreciative gaze skimmed over her sundress. "What seems to be the problem?"

"Well, if I knew that, I wouldn't be standing on the side of the road baking in the sun, now would I? It coughed and jerked a few times and then it just quit."

"Want me to give it a try, or would that be stepping on your toes?"

Oh, he was so smug. She wanted to stamp her feet. Or slug him.

Instead, not bothering to hide her irritation, she gestured toward the driver's door. "Be my guest, macho man."

He slid inside and turned the ignition. The engine cranked over but didn't catch. Getting back out, tossing the keys up and catching them in his hand, he said blandly, "You're out of gas."

"I am not out of gas," she said, exasperated with this whole sorry mess. "Figures I'd get rescued by somebody who knows even less about cars than I do. I just filled the tank two days ago."

His smile faded and his eyes sharpened. "That gas gauge is sitting past empty, Penny."

"Well, maybe the damn thing's broke. If I was out

of gas, one of those idiot lights should have come on." She snatched the keys from him, checked the gauge herself. Still not satisfied, she got out and tugged a pussy willow from the ditch by the side of the road, unscrewed the gas cap and threaded the reed down into the tank. When she pulled it out, the stem was barely damp at the tip.

Turning, she frowned at Joe. He wasn't smiling.

"Somebody siphoned the gas out of my car."

"Where did you park it?"

"Smack-dab on Main Street. In front of the bookstore."

"And before that?"

"In the driveway at home."

"And between the gas station and home and the bookstore, you haven't been anywhere else?"

"I'd have said so if I had." That meant someone had been lurking outside her house after Joe had gone home last night. Chills walked up her spine.

"Damn it, Penny. This is starting to bug me. Someone rifles your house and now steals your gas."

"You don't think it bugs me?"

"Do you have *any* idea who could be doing this?"

"No. If I did, you'd be the first to know." They weren't going to solve anything standing on the side of the road in the sweltering heat. "I don't suppose you happen to have a spare can of gas on you?"

He shook his head. "Used it in Emmett's tractor the other day and didn't get around to replacing it."

"Then it appears I need to hitch a ride to the filling station."

"I'll call and get someone out here to dust for prints."

"Don't bother."

"Penny—"

"I wiped the car down this morning, Joe." Solid black with wider than standard tires, shiny rims and darkly tinted windows, the Cadillac looked like a dangerous panther on the prowl. She was sure there was a law written somewhere that a vehicle like that should be kept gleaming.

He let out a breath. "Let's go, then."

Penny retrieved her purse, her laptop computer and her attaché case from the Caddie. Locking the doors, she transferred everything to the squad car and got in.

It was a moment before she realized Joe hadn't started the car, that he was simply staring at her with an enigmatic expression on his face.

"What?"

"What's in the case?"

"A forty-five and a couple of extra clips."

"Any treasures in that purse?"

"Of course." She patted the black pocket that held the thirty-eight. "You're not going to ask if I have a permit, are you?"

He shook his head, the corner of his mouth twitching. In his eyes was something soft and admiring. It sent a flutter of butterflies in her stomach.

"Looks like you're armed to the teeth."

"You could say that. Or that I'm well prepared to take care of myself."

He reached for the squad car's ignition. "Too bad you don't seem to have a gun on your person when the situation calls for it. Which is a good thing," he added when she bristled. "Messy things having to fill out all those reports when people go around shooting each other."

He was referring to the night of the break-in when she'd been out running. And the night she'd arrived in town and they'd tussled. "If you don't quit gloating, Colter, I'm going to shoot *you*. And I'd think you'd consider yourself lucky I wasn't armed the night you jumped me."

He winked at her. "Very lucky. So how did the grand opening at the bookstore go?"

"Fabulous."

He looked over at her. "And?"

"And what?"

"What *aren't* you telling me?"

A smile started from deep inside her and grew. "Does the bank president sit on the city council?"

"Yes."

"That's what I thought." She fiddled with her purse. "I sort of scared his daughter. I imagine she'll complain."

Joe tried to keep from laughing as Penny told him about her run-in with Lanie. Lanie Dubois was prissy and fake and more often than not, mean-spirited. It would do her good to be put in her place.

He wished he'd been there to see it. Penny in action was something else. Even in a silky sundress that skimmed her curves and ended at midthigh, she radiated mystery and capability.

She'd make a hell of a partner. A life partner.

The thought didn't even jolt him. He'd spent a lot

of time last night thinking about that very thing. But thinking and coming up with a workable way to make that happen were two entirely different breeds of cattle. He had to face the very real possibility that despite what he wanted deep in his heart, it might not be possible.

The fact that she so easily packed a gun was testament. Penny had a career and it wasn't here in the tiny town of Darby.

The dispatcher's voice over the radio interrupted his thoughts. He lifted the mike. "This is Joe, Karen. Go ahead."

"Ty Mason just called in to report his pickup stolen."

Joe looked in his rearview mirror. "Green Ford, short bed, nineteen ninety-three or four?"

"Nineteen ninety-four." Karen gave the license number. "Have you seen it?"

"Passed me a few minutes ago." Even as he said it, he was slowing the squad car, pulling a U-turn on the highway. He glanced at Penny. "This is really bad timing. I shouldn't even think of starting a pursuit with a civilian in the car."

Her jaw actually dropped. "A civil…?" She rolled her eyes. "Get real, would you?" Even as she said the words, she was testing the buckle on her seat belt, grabbing her fancy laptop out of the case, all but rubbing her hands together in glee. "I've got a security clearance so high it'd make your nose bleed. Hammer down, Colter. You're not going to catch anybody driving like a granny."

He might have known she'd enjoy something like

this. And he might have asked her why she had her computer out, but he needed all his concentration because the kids in the pickup had just realized they'd been made.

"Damn it, they're running." He spoke into the mike, gave his coordinates to Karen and hit the sirens and lights.

"Come on, baby, hurry up," Penny murmured.

"I've got it to the floor," he said tightly. "If you're going to back-seat drive and criticize I'll let you out."

"Oh, settle down. I wasn't talking to you."

He started to point out that they were the only two people in the car, but the suspect vehicle made a sharp right turn into a trailer park and it took all his concentration to make the turn without spinning out. He saw the taillights disappear around a turn.

"Watch the baby!" Penny screamed.

He jerked the wheel, tapped the brakes when every reflex he possessed urged him to stomp. The car swerved but he kept it under control. His insides were another matter. His knees turned to water as a frightened mother snatched the child off his tricycle and up in her arms.

Joe slowed his speed. He'd just as soon let the thieves go rather than endanger more lives. "Damn it, I hate this."

"You're doing fine."

He nearly laughed. He didn't have enough spit to do it.

"Take a right."

He obeyed without question.

"Now left."

He took his eyes off the empty road in front of him long enough to glance at Penny. If he didn't see a vehicle, what the heck was she looking at?

Her eyes were glued to her computer, her fingers hovering over the mouse. It was a compact, stream-lined unit with a small antenna extended up from the side.

"Navigational system," she said without taking her eyes from the screen. "You watch the road, I'll watch the map."

"Yes ma'am."

"There are two of them."

"Computer tell you that?"

"Mmm. Heat sensor."

"Does it tell you their names, too?"

"Cute, Joe. They're turning left. Uh-oh."

"Uh-oh, what?"

"They stopped."

"So I see." The green pickup, still rocking, was half in and half out of the ditch. The two boys took off on foot through the thicket of trees. Joe lifted the mike, gave their location. "Suspects are on foot, Karen. I'm in pursuit."

"Ten-four, Joe. Darren's on his way to back you up."

He started to jump out of the car and give chase.

Penny grabbed his shirt sleeve. "Not so fast, Chief. Let's do this the easy way, shall we?" She studied her screen. "There's a road just on the other side of these trees. It'll save you time and grief if you just drive around." She glanced up at him and smiled sweetly. "Unless of course you're in the mood for a sweaty run in the humidity?"

"Smart aleck." He shook his head and put the car in Reverse.

Penny laughed. "You're just jealous because I have better toys than you do."

"Damn right. So, how do you know they'll come out on the other side? Maybe they'll go left or right."

"Not according to the computer. Two little blips right here, heading straight for..." she paused, peered at the area map on the screen, "Wiley Springs Road."

Trusting Penny completely, he gave dispatch the new information, then asked, "Why aren't the trees blocking your sensor?"

"This is a new device with all kinds of trick equipment. The program's designed to bounce the signal off a satellite. Up, then down. Much better range and accuracy that way."

He glanced at her as he pulled to a stop on Wiley Springs Road. "You're pretty handy to have around, 007."

"Me? Or my gadgets?"

His look was very direct, and very intimate. It pleased him when she lost some of her composure. "You. The gadgets are a bonus."

He was out of the car, leaning his hip against the hood, a pair of handcuffs dangling from his finger when the two young boys burst out of the thicket. With twin looks of bewilderment, they skidded to a halt, chests heaving.

"Afternoon Chad. Sean. Y'all want to come on over here and slip your wrists in my bracelets?"

The boys hung their heads and came forward. They weren't bad kids, just adventuresome.

About that time, another squad car pulled up.

"What have we got?" Darren asked.

"Couple of joyriders. Have Karen put a call into Ty Mason. Tell him to come pick up his boys at the station. Then run them in for me, would you?"

"Sure thing, Chief."

Joe turned to Chad Mason. "You boys study driver's ed in school?"

"Yes, sir."

"They teach you what to do when a police officer signals with sirens and lights?"

"Yes, sir."

"Must have been sleeping that day and the lesson didn't stick, hmm?"

"No, sir."

"Your daddy reported his truck stolen. Next time, ask for the keys, why don't you. And another piece of advice. When a police officer falls in behind you, don't run. You just never know when a cop's had a bad day. An officer gets in a pursuit and adrenaline starts to flow. He's scared for his life, doesn't know what he's gonna find when he makes the stop. Innocent people can get hurt."

The boys were beginning to shake. Good.

"You're lucky it was me who stopped you and not some other agency. See that beautiful woman over there?" The boys nodded. "Don't let the appearance fool you. Government agent. Deadeye aim. She's packing more heat than I've seen in a while. Wouldn't want to tangle with her."

The boys shook their heads, looked at Penny, scared spitless.

Joe grinned and ambled back over to the car.

Penny was frowning.

"What in the world did you tell those boys?"

"That you liked to shoot people."

WHEN PENNY finally got home after putting gas in the car, the aunts were sitting on their porch—with shotguns resting across their knees.

Oh, this would never do.

She closed her eyes for a moment, took a breath, then got out of the car and headed across the street.

Everybody was determined to guard her.

Mounting the porch steps, she looked pointedly at the weapons. "Are we expecting a siege?"

"We heard about somebody taking gasoline out of your car, and we're making sure the varmints don't think they can sneak over here and clean you out while you're stranded. Sister and I are sure that was the plan."

"How in the world did you hear about my gas being siphoned?"

"Loralie Vanna."

"The telephone operator?"

"Told you she was a nosy one, but in this case I'll not judge her harshly. Though in my day, I didn't call all and sundry when I overheard a conversation."

"What conversation did she overhear?"

"Oh, she didn't actually overhear it. She's been steppin' out with old Floyd Mylar over at the filling station, and he told her about you coming in with Joe needing gasoline when you'd just been in day before yesterday and bought a whole tank full. Loralie called and asked if we'd seen who took the gas from your car. Tried to pass her questions off as sleuthing, but it was clear in her tone that she was tickled to know a story before Sister and I did."

"Fool woman's still trying to fill Georgia's shoes," Wanetta said. "Everybody knows Georgia was the best operator this town had."

"Of course," Penny said. "Still, it's probably not a good idea to sit outside so blatantly armed."

"Why in the world not? Just as well to head off trouble before it gets here, don't you think?"

"Yes, but we should be a bit more discreet, not tip our hand quite so easily."

"Oh, you do have a point, dear. The element of surprise. Criminals would never think to suspect two old ladies of packing heat."

Penny made every effort to keep a straight face. But despite the urge to laugh, she was genuinely worried.

"Aunt Georgia, I think these are just kids' pranks. Joe said there's a group of delinquents running around town whose parents are turning a blind eye. Stolen money and gasoline are petty things. I don't want to see you all get in the middle of something and get hurt. I'd never forgive myself."

"But you need protection, dear."

She hated to lie, but these were extenuating circumstances. "I'm a pretty tough cookie. Besides that, Joe's coming to stay, with me." Lest they go off on a romantic tangent, she added, "It's all very cut-and-dried. Just two law enforcement agencies joining forces.''

''Always thought the two of you would make a good team,'' Wanetta said, her gaze sharpening. ''He broke your heart once, though. I'd not like to see him do it again.''

Penny smiled a little sadly. ''Maybe I'll break his.''

''I think you could,'' Georgia said.

''I hope not.'' When she'd first come to town, she might have taken some pleasure in making Joe Colter want her, then jerking the rug from beneath him. Revenge.

But there was no pleasure in deliberately hurting the man you loved.

That wasn't to say she was going to get involved with him.

Even though she had a million things to do in the house, Penny spent a good part of the afternoon visiting with Georgia and Wanetta on the porch, sipping iced tea and laughing over crazy stories of the town's people...and learning about her grandmother's life.

Then suddenly Georgia bobbed to her feet and snatched up the shotgun she'd leaned against the house, cradling the twenty-gauge rigidly in her crossed arms. ''Here we go.''

Penny quickly adjusted the barrel which was pointing straight at Wanetta. It wouldn't do for Georgia to accidentally discharge her firearm into her sister's chest.

Turning, she looked across the street to see what had caused the stir. Nathan's rental car was parked at the curb in front of her house and he was getting out.

"Easy ladies. He's a friend." For some reason, she didn't want to explain Nathan's connection to her grandmother. The unrequited love affair between their grandparents had obviously etched deep scars on both Agnes and Al. Perhaps in death, they were now joined. In any case, Penny felt it important to guard their privacy.

"Please," she said with every ounce of entreaty she could muster. "Put the guns away. For me?"

The aunts nodded and Penny relaxed a bit, kissed each of their cheeks, and started to move off the porch.

"Joe won't like another man courting you, you know."

She paused, jolted, but recovered with barely a beat. "Joe doesn't have much to say about who courts me, now does he?"

Nathan was waiting for her at the curb when she got across the street.

"I came by to see if I could collect on that rain check for dinner. Whoa, what happened to your head?" Gently, he brushed her hair aside, looked at the healing wound, compassion in his green eyes.

He smelled very nice, Penny thought. And looked very nice, in an ivy league sort of way. Too bad he didn't make her heart stutter and her breath hitch.

Penny smiled. At least Nathan didn't know her background or view her as some sort of mysterious town heroine. The only thing he knew about her was that she was Agnes's granddaughter. She had no secret agent stories to live down or up to.

"I got conked in the head by a piece of wood

harder than my head.'' She'd leave it at that. For all he knew, the attic stairs could have fallen on her.

''Ouch. I'm glad you're okay.''

''Me, too. Did you find the hotel okay?''

''Actually, I drove on over to Austin and spent a couple days visiting with a college buddy.'' His gaze dropped to her silk dress. It wasn't a leer, just masculine appreciation that gave Penny's feminine ego a boost. ''I confess, though. You kept popping into my mind.''

''How rude of me.''

He grinned. ''Absolutely. So I figured I'd come on back by, see if I could persuade you to have that dinner with me.''

She glanced over when another vehicle pulled up, this one turning into her driveway.

Joe.

Joe won't like another man courting you.

By the look on his face as he got out of the car and came toward them, that was an understatement. His gaze was pinned on Nathan, filled with suspicion and a silent warning that any man with half a brain would recognize.

A warning that clearly said: ''Back off, she's mine.''

The fact that he *was* acting like a dog with a bone made Penny feel just a touch ornery.

''Joe Colter, let me introduce you to Nathan Lantrelle,'' she said when he'd stopped next to them on the porch. Odd that she had yet to invite Nathan inside.

When the men shook hands, she added, ''Nathan

and I were just on our way to dinner.'' Both of them looked at her with a bit of surprise. Joe because she was going despite his muscle flexing, and Nathan because she'd accepted without telling him first.

"Was there something you needed, Joe?"

His eyes locked onto hers, held. "Yes. There's something I need." His voice was deep and very, very soft. "It'll wait."

It was both a threat and a promise. It turned her insides to a quivering mass of nerves...and anticipation.

Chapter Nine

Penny left Nathan sitting in his car after dinner and waved from the porch as he reluctantly drove away. She knew he wanted to come in with her, but she just couldn't talk herself into extending the evening.

A boring evening.

An evening where Nathan had wanted to talk about the house and their grandparents and the type of items people save, and all she could think about was the look in Joe's eyes.

It'll wait.

Obviously *he* hadn't. She'd half expected to see his truck still sitting in the driveway, cursed herself for the pang of disappointment when it wasn't. Now that all was said and done, she regretted giving in to the ornery streak that had prodded her into going out with Nathan when what she really wanted was to spend time with Joe.

Although, it *was* rather flattering that Nathan appeared taken with her.

She put her key in the doorknob, then realized it wasn't locked. She'd been so caught up in the drama of the two men on the porch, she'd gone off without securing the house.

She wasn't going to beat herself up too bad over the lack of caution. Joe had been standing there, too. And *he* obviously hadn't thought to twist the lock on the door, either. Still, she eased the gun out of her purse.

"Have a good time?"

Fright gave her a head rush that roared in her ears. She had her arm extended and gun aimed in a matter of seconds.

Joe held up his hands. "Deadeye *and* a quick draw. Impressive."

Penny pointed the thirty-eight toward the ceiling, flicked back on the safety. "Damn it, Joe. One of these days I really *am* going to shoot you. Where is your truck?"

He got to his feet, totally undisturbed by her threat. The look on his face made her heart pound.

Anger mixed with passion.

A very dangerous combination.

"In your garage. I didn't want the neighbors to talk."

"If you'd just gone home they wouldn't have anything to talk about."

With each step forward he took, she took one back. She wasn't used to this side of Joe, and she suddenly felt very cowardly.

She glanced around, seeking a distraction. "Where's Scout?" The puppy should have come running the minute she came in the door. Definitely not a watchdog.

"I shut him in the kitchen. He was making a mess out of a photo album." He kept coming toward her.

"Oh."

"You didn't answer my question. Did you have a good time?"

She tilted her chin, glared at him. "Fabulous."

"Liar." He paused when her back hit the wall. "You thought about me, didn't you?"

He was practically on top of her, looking down at her like a man with a dire purpose.

And Penny felt that same purpose. Urgently.

"Get over yourself, Colter."

"That's not my problem. My problem is getting over *you.*" He wrapped his hands around her upper arms, lifted her nearly off her toes and lowered his mouth to hers. Given the barely checked emotions she could clearly see simmering, she expected aggression.

She got gentleness.

It was her undoing.

Years of frustration and a lifetime of wanting seemed to pour from that kiss.

My problem is getting over you.

Could that really be true? She was a much different woman than the girl who'd left here sixteen years ago. Oh, she still had insecurities, but at the moment they were hidden behind a sexy dress, skillfully applied makeup and a sassy attitude. And the two sides of her were getting confused. She felt as though any minute now, someone was going to say, "Will the real Penny please stand up."

And that wouldn't be the Penny Joe was responding to.

But she was simply too caught up in the moment—and in the man—to care.

He drew back scant inches, let her feet rest back on the floor, rubbed his hands up and down her arms.

"I said I could wait, but I don't think I can. I want you more than I ever knew I could want a woman. I could have killed Lantrelle when he walked away with you."

"I know." Her heart was pounding in earnest now.

"You did it deliberately."

"Yes."

He shifted so that her thighs were practically straddling his knee. "It's like you put a spell on me and I'm helpless to get out from under it."

"Do you want to?" She licked her lips. "Get out from under it, that is."

He shook his head. "I want to make love with you."

She was about to take the biggest step—or make the biggest mistake—of her life. "Then why don't you?"

His lips twitched slightly. "Since you can likely outshoot me and inflict injury in combat, I'd like to hear you say, yes."

"*Likely?* I already proved I'm a better shot." She sucked in a breath when he propped one hand on the wall behind her and used the knuckles of his other hand to lightly, carelessly, rub back and forth over the swell of her breasts above the scoop neck of her dress, his gaze steady on hers.

"We haven't gone two out of three, yet." Joe moved his hand up her throat, rested his fingers against her jaw, tipped her head back even farther. "I've still got a few moves you haven't seen." He watched her eyes go hot with arousal, saw her chest rise and fall in a deep breath of surrender.

"Show me," she whispered.

The invitation was all he'd been waiting for. Although he was deliberately crowding her, taunting her, Joe felt his hands tremble. She smelled like a tropical island and felt like the finest silk.

And she kissed him like a woman utterly sure of her femininity and her effect on a man...or a woman simply swept away. He liked the idea that he could consume her, feel that hot edge of hunger as she moaned deep in her throat and poured herself into a kiss that left him numb.

Memories assailed him, of another time, another room where the sultry air had burned his lungs as a brown-eyed vixen had emerged from a nondescript cocoon into a vibrantly alive, stunning butterfly. She'd turned his world inside out sixteen years ago, and she was doing the same to him today.

He slipped his hand under the hem of her dress and pushed it upward, aching to feel the silk of bare skin.

The stiffening was slight, but Joe was so acutely attuned to every humming inch of her that he noticed.

"Easy."

She rested her forehead against his. "It's been a long time."

"How long?"

She just looked at him.

"How long, baby? I don't want to hurt you."

"Sixteen years."

His breath rushed out in a whoosh. "Sixteen—you haven't...?"

She shook her head.

Now more than ever, he knew he had to be careful with her. With her chin lifted and her eyes nearly spitting a challenge, she was telling him he'd been her first and only lover.

She humbled him. She was so confident, appeared to need no one, tried so hard to act tough. But there was a vulnerability beneath the toned body, well-defined arms, sassy mouth and mysterious eyes. She could be absolutely no-nonsense one minute, then be cutting up the next.

And then, she could stand there with her heart in her eyes, telling him he was the luckiest man on earth, the only man she'd ever let close.

He'd screwed up the first time. He would take care this time. Great care.

Bending at the knees, he lifted her in his arms.

"Joe!"

"Shh. Let me." He took her into the bedroom, lowered her to her feet beside the bed, switched on the lamp so that soft light fell across the room. He wanted to see her. Every inch of her.

He gently kissed her temple, then the injury on her head that still twisted his gut when he let himself imagine what could have been. Reaching behind her for the zipper of her dress, he lowered it slowly, eased the straps off her shoulders, kissed the swell of her breasts as the dress fell to a puddle at her feet.

He sucked in a stunned breath.

Her barely-there panties were electric blue satin

held only by tiny bows. One tug and they'd fall away. Her bra was of the same matching satin, strapless, pushing her small breasts into plump mounds above the sexy material.

Who would have known that Penny Archer would wear heart-stopping lingerie?

He stepped back and looked at her for a very long moment. "You take my breath away."

"I…" She raised her hands to the bra. Modesty and uncertainty flickered in her eyes. "It's always been my weakness. I can't resist sexy lingerie."

"I, for one, am very glad. Let me look." He circled her wrists, lowered her hands. "You're such a contrast. Tough steel and denim. In-your-face and lethal with a right hook or a weapon. And so sexy and feminine you make a man's knees dissolve."

Her chest rose and fell, her eyes dilated with passion. "Well, before yours dissolve, could you use them to get a little closer?"

"Yes, ma'am." He'd thought to ease them into the moment, build on it, but before he could even give a nod to coherency, he was lost in the touch of her hands. They raced over his body, tugging his shirt over his head, fumbling with the snap of his jeans. She pressed against him as though trying to become one, leaving him aching and whirling and off balance.

His good intentions to take care nearly vanished under the sensual onslaught. He managed to get his jeans off despite Penny's hands tangling with his, helping, urging him faster.

They were both athletic individuals. One of them needed to display a little caution here.

"Wait, baby hold on—"

Her lips cut off his words. Man alive, he couldn't even think straight. He was caught in a vortex of wonder and sensation that bordered on madness.

"Joe." She panted. "Touch me. More."

To hell with caution.

With his body humming, he laid her on the bed and did just as she'd asked, giving them both more pleasure that he'd thought was possible.

He was going to take his time even if it killed him.... Because Penny Archer was a woman a man should savor.

And it could very well kill him—or drive him mad. With even the lightest stroke of his fingertips, the barest hint of pressure, she responded like a flash of gun powder under the sparks of a flint. Shyness gave way to trust as she let him have his way with her body.

She'd given him the gift of herself sixteen years ago.

She was giving it to him again today.

He wanted it for the rest of his life but knew he'd scare her off if he said so.

So he let his lips and his hands and his body do the talking for him, using every ounce of skill and control he possessed.

She writhed beneath him, wrapped those strong legs around his waist, touched him everywhere she could reach, her hands feverish.

He nearly went mad with desire. This is how he remembered her. Hot and sweet and wild.

She didn't apologize for her ardor, didn't hide behind modesty or expect him to do all the work—although he was trying like crazy to do just that.

He wanted to *give* to Penny. All that he had to give. To leave his memory etched on her brain, his touch stamped on her skin so that every time she drew a breath or closed her eyes she would think of him.

Like he'd thought of her these past years.

Sliding down her body, he anointed her perfectly shaped breasts with open-mouth kisses, saw her stomach quiver when he ran his tongue down the center of her flat belly, watched her back arch off the bed when he pressed his lips to her in the most intimate kiss a man could give a woman.

"Joe!" Penny was certain she was going to come apart. She was awash in so many sensations she couldn't identify a single one. Nearly incoherent, all she could do was ride out the storm.

The air in the room pulsated with need and hunger. She writhed, clutched at his shoulders, urged him back up her body and rolled with him, determined to take that final step herself.

He cupped the back of her thighs, shook his head. "Uh-uh."

She was pleased to hear the unsteadiness in his voice, then stunned when he flipped her to her back.

She couldn't help it—she giggled. "Are we going to make love here or fight about it?"

"Give me about three seconds, and I'll show you." Holding her steady, he reached for his wallet and took out a condom.

She was on the pill—doctor's orders to regulate her periods—but she dropped a hot kiss on his shoulder for his thoughtfulness of providing protection, and not assuming.

But gratitude fled from her mind as he swept her back into a passion so strong she nearly wept. With his lips and hands he brought her to yet another peak, then pushed her legs apart with his knee and clamped his hands on her hips to hold her still.

She opened her eyes, confused to find herself anchored to the bed when every instinct she possessed cried out for movement. She was restless, on fire. She needed…

At last he tilted her hips and entered her, pushing forward slowly, carefully, watching her.

When he eased back, she sucked in a breath, grabbed for him.

''Okay?'' His jaw was tight and sweat trickled down his temple.

''Better than okay. I won't break, Joe.'' He was holding back his own pleasure for fear of hurting her.

She could have told him he was light years away from hurting her.

Physically, at least.

She felt the fullness of him, stretching her, barely inside her. Cupping her hands over his firm buttocks, she gave them both what they desperately wanted, pulling him into her until there was no way to tell where one left off and the other began.

''Penny—''

''Don't talk.'' Oh, it was good. So good. And it had been so long.

Only Joe could make her feel this way, make her mind go blank and her body catch fire. There was nowhere to hide, no *way* to hide. Emotions were laid wide open, swept along by a passion so exquisitely stunning, she felt her eyes go damp.

She cried out in triumph as he drove into her, hard and deep. Before, he'd treated her as though she were fragile china. Now, he demanded with a ruthlessness that she was more than willing to match.

The climax curled in her belly, dark and desperate. So close...

"Let go, baby. I'm here."

And she did let go. Reached for the pleasure that only Joe had ever given her, held on, and rode it through every violent, shuddering crest into oblivion.

"WHO WON?" Penny asked when she'd recovered enough breath to do so.

"I did."

She sputtered out a giggle and lightly pinched his chest. She'd expected him to admit it was a draw.

"Well, I did," he said softly. "I won the girl."

Oh, why did he have to say sweet things like that? The emotions that washed over Penny were so bittersweet she wanted to weep.

She'd been in love with Joe all her life. But something was always standing in their way. Social class, an adolescent bet, his marriage, time and distance. Now was no different.

She desperately wanted this man, but couldn't allow herself to have him—because she couldn't be the woman to give him his dream. She couldn't give him those children he wanted to fill that big white house to carry on his legacy. She just couldn't risk it. The memories of her mother were as vivid and fresh as though the hotel incident had happened only yesterday.

"Have I finally surprised you out of a snappy comeback?" he asked.

"Don't gloat, Colter. It's not nice." Restless, wanting more than she knew she could have, she asked, "Did you eat dinner?"

"No, my date went out with someone else."

"Wasn't very nice of her, was it?" She sat up and reached for a silky robe at the foot of the bed, threading her arms through it.

"Hey, come back here."

He made a grab for her, but she eluded him. Lying in bed next to Joe was causing way too many foolish fantasies. She needed to appear sophisticated, a little aloof—to continue the act. Because if she let herself just *be,* she was terribly afraid she'd become needy— like the starstruck girl in high school whose heart had swelled with hope when the most popular boy had singled her out.

"Since I made you miss a meal, the least I can do is feed you."

He got up and put on his jeans. "I never argue with a woman offering food. Besides, we wouldn't want my stamina to wane so early in the evening."

Her knees nearly dissolved. With a mere look, Joe Colter could turn simple words into an exquisitely thrilling sensual threat.

Well, why not? She thought. Would it be so wrong to let herself enjoy Joe while she was here? Would it be so bad to wipe away the blot of a silly bet and start over? Just two consenting adults having an adult relationship—a temporary one.

Before she could get out of the room, the phone rang. Changing course, she went to the nightstand and picked up the receiver.

"Hello?"

Nothing. Chills raised the hair on her arms. She could hear someone breathing, could hear a faint swishing sound she couldn't quite identify. Kind of like the dead air between songs on a CD.

Tape recorder? She wondered. But why?

After what seemed like endless moments, the silent caller hung up. She depressed the disconnect button, then picked up her cell phone and immediately punched in another number, a little surprised to note that her hands were shaking.

She glanced at Joe who'd gone absolutely still. The intensity in his eyes telegraphed danger, but without an ounce of sexual teasing.

The line at the Texas Confidential headquarters was picked up halfway through the first ring and Penny tore her gaze away from Joe. He made it difficult to concentrate.

"Kendra, it's Penny. Any luck on tracing my grandmother's phone lines?"

"I've gone over it from every line and connection. It's clear, Penny. There are no taps or bugs in place— other than mine, that is. The noises you're hearing could be a message machine set on record, or a portable recorder, but nothing sophisticated."

Penny could hear computer keys tapping. Kendra Alvarez was an ace hacker. Whatever a person could imagine, Kendra could do it or find it or accomplish it with her computer. Thank goodness she was on the good guy's side.

"Damn," Kendra said. "I'm hooked into your line but I can't get a fix on that last call. I'm sorry, Penny. Try to keep them on the phone longer, next time."

"I should have known that." Penny glanced at Joe, aware that he was listening to her side of the conversation, practically spitting bullets to find out what the heck was going on.

"It's tough to think straight when you're flustered," Kendra consoled. "Oh, hang on a minute. Mitchell's about to rip the phone out of my hand."

Penny smiled, easing a bit. She could picture Mitchell Forbes, sixty-five, handsome and fit, leaning on his silver-handled cane that he used more for show than out of necessity, and flicking his silver lighter. A gesture that gave away emotions he never showed the outside world.

"Penny," Mitchell said. "What the hell is going on out there?"

"Hello to you, too, Mitchell," she said softly. She'd only been gone two weeks but she missed the man who was like a father to her. "How are you feeling?" Although it had been seven months since Mitchell's heart attack and surgery, the illness had shaken her terribly and she still worried.

"I'm feeling fine. Now I want to know why the agents are calling meetings, grilling each other on any loose ends that might not have been tied up with Rialto, hanging all over Kendra's computer every time the alarm goes off."

"Alarm?"

"She's got it rigged to alert her when your phone rings."

"She's a gem, Mitchell. We're lucky Rafe had the good sense to hold on to her."

"Yes. You're being evasive."

Penny sighed. "It's just a creepy feeling I've got."

"Come on, Penny. You're smarter than that. Kendra told us about the break-in."

"I wish everyone would quit worrying about me. It's only a little bump." She realized her mistake instantly. Not only did the mention of her wound cause Joe to take a step closer, it sent Mitchell's voice up an octave. A rare occurrence.

"You were injured? Why wasn't I told about this—"

"Mitchell, I'm fine. Now do you want to hear the facts as I know them or not?"

"Ever efficient. Yes, I do."

So she put the information in chronological order for him, starting with that first phone call where no one would speak, the break-in at county records, the adolescents seen running across the town square, and then the break-in at her house.

"The intruder was coming out as I was coming in and the door caught me in the head," she explained, glancing once again at Joe, hating constantly having to relive that embarrassing show of ineptness. "A small amount of money was taken and my belongings were rifled and strewn about, but there was no malicious destruction. Which leads me to believe it wasn't kids. Then yesterday, someone siphoned the gas out of my car.''

"That's it. I'm sending the guys down there.''

"Mitchell, no! I've—'' She wished Joe wasn't standing there listening so intently. She intended to tell him the whole truth about her job, but she wanted to choose her time and her words. Not have him deduce it himself based on an overheard telephone conversation. "I've got backup.''

"Who?''

"Joe Colter.''

There was silence on the line. No creepy noises this time. Just the pregnant pause of a man with a sharp-as-a-tack mind who'd known her all her adult life. "You trust him to back you up?''

The question went much deeper than the obvious of being handy with a gun. "Yes. He's the chief of police here in Darby. He's qualified.''

"You know what I'm saying.''

"I know what you're saying,'' she repeated. *Do you trust him not to break your heart again.* "Keep the guys there, Mitchell.''

"I hope I won't regret this.''

"You won't. But there is something you can do for me. I might need a locator.''

"For what?''

"There's a man named Don Gilard. He's recently been paroled from the state prison, ex-husband of a friend of mine. Abusive. She put him there, and I've a gut feeling he'll be back.''

He paused, then asked bluntly, "Is this your fight?''

"Absolutely." Janelle was a friend. And Penny had come to realize how vitally important friendships were to her.

She had connections to provide extra protection and she was going to use them. And she knew without a doubt that Mitchell would lend her those resources whether he approved or not. He trusted and relied on her judgment, which very often in the past had meant the difference between life and death.

"I know of a man in Austin," Mitchell said.

"I'll let you know if I need him. So far Gilard's checking in with his parole officer." At least he had been a couple of days ago when Joe had inquired. "Take care, Mitchell. And don't worry about me."

"Then you call in daily."

"I'll call." She hung up the phone without actually agreeing to the *daily* part.

When she turned, her heart skipped a beat. Joe stood two feet away, chest and feet bare, jeans riding low on his hips. Sensuality, concern and irritation radiated from him like a volcano preparing to erupt.

"You didn't tell me about the phone calls." Although his voice was whisper soft, it was taut as razor wire.

"Slipped my mind."

His expression told her he didn't believe that for a minute.

"I'll move some things in tomorrow."

"Joe—"

"This isn't negotiable, so don't give me any sass. I'm staying here until we get to the bottom of whatever's going on. We're both in the business of tracking clues, so the two of us together in one place will get the job done better.''

"That doesn't mean you have to move in. Besides, isn't this branding season or something?''

"The ranch has a full summer crew and my dad as ramrod. I'm not needed there and, damn it, I'm not going to argue about this with you." He raked a hand through his hair. "We're a team, Penny. You just said so yourself to your boss.''

"Are you saying you want to stick together twenty-four hours a day?''

"If it becomes necessary, that's what we'll do.''

Despite the fact that she liked having Joe here, a flash of temper made her snap. "I've told you before, I don't need or want a baby-sitter so don't try to pull that bossiness on me. I won't put up with it.''

He stepped up to her. "Did I say anything about baby-sitting?''

"Your tone implied it.''

"Then I apologize for my tone." He bent his knees and kissed the chin she'd jutted out. "Let's do this together, Pen. All these unanswered questions. I'm worried…and not as a law enforcement officer. This is personal.''

He cupped her face in his hands and tenderly pressed his lips against her forehead. Just that.

The unspoken emotion in that simple gesture shook Penny to her core.

Oh, God, she really did have the power to hurt him. Her own pain, she could deal with. Could she handle his, too? Could she convince herself that he would get over it, would come to see that she'd done him a favor by not staying?

Yes, she had to believe that. When he had those happy children bouncing around his knee, carrying on the Colter name, he would thank her.

"So are we a team?" He *asked* this time. That made her smile.

"Might as well be. Otherwise Georgia and Wanetta will go back to toting shotguns out on the porch."

"Oh, man. Tell me they didn't."

"Okay, they didn't." At his raised brows she said, "Just following orders, Chief."

"The day you follow my orders, is the day pigs are going to soar all the way to the moon."

"You never know. That could happen."

"Pigs flying or you obeying orders?"

She put her hand on his chest, felt the warm, taut skin beneath her palm, the beat of his heart.

If someone had a beef with her for reasons unknown, Joe could well be in the line of fire. She hated that she might be putting him in danger, but knew he'd never budge from her side. She'd stand on her head naked in a blizzard if it meant saving his life.

"When it counts, Joe, I'll always come through for you." She said it softly, seriously.

"Will you?" he asked just as softly.

"As your backup."

"As my partner?"

Just as Mitchell had earlier, Joe was asking a much deeper question. A personal question that had little to do with her guarding his blind side with a gun, and a lot to do with their future.

There were so many things she wanted to say, couldn't say.

She gave him back another statement that weighed so heavy with unspoken meaning. ''I don't want you hurt.''

Silence stretched for an eon.

Rather than keep up the parry of innuendo, he simply lifted her in his arms, and pressed his lips to hers in a soul-stirring kiss that spoke from the heart as he carried her back to bed.

Chapter Ten

"You know it's the talk of the town that you're shacking up with Joe Colter." Kelly Robertson slathered on scented hand cream, then passed the jar back to Janelle.

"Pity we have to hear such news from the town rather than our best friend," Pam said, pushing her cuticles back with an orangewood stick.

Penny sighed and looked at her friends, all of them sitting around a Formica table in the corner of Janelle's beauty shop. The smell of hair dye and nail solvent permeated the air even though there was no business being conducted—other than four friends giving each other manicures. Penny's short nails now sported a shiny coat of clear polish. She'd probably have it chipped off in a day.

"We're not shacking up. He's just got some ridiculous idea that I need protection. It's been a week and not a single thing has happened here. The man's paranoid."

"And in love," Pam commented.

Penny jerked and glared at her friend. "Don't start with that."

"Oh, get off it. You and Joe make a perfect couple. What's the big deal in admitting it."

"I'm not staying. You guys know that." She reached up and pushed her hair behind her ear before she remembered that her nails were still wet. "Damn it."

"Here," Kelly said, reaching across for Penny's hand. "I'll fix it." She gave a discreet squeeze and Penny felt a lump form in her throat. She and Kelly were the closest. There was unspoken understanding between them.

"How's the packing coming?" Kelly asked, swiping a cotton ball soaked in acetate over the smudged nail.

"Boxes are sealed and stacked for storage. I intended to have a yard sale, but everything I picked up I ended up packing. There's not enough left over to bother with. I know it doesn't make any sense, but I just couldn't get rid of Grandmother's stuff."

"Memories are treasures," Janelle said with a soft smile. "Some of them at least."

Penny reached over with her free hand and covered Janelle's, gave a squeeze much the same as Kelly had done to her moments ago.

"So what's happening with the preppy guy?" Pam asked. "Nathan, right?"

"He's called a couple of times this week, but I told him I was too busy and didn't have room for a social life." She shrugged and tried to keep her hands flat so she wouldn't smudge her nail polish. "I assume he went back home."

"And took his gramps's love letters with him."

Although she was reluctant to discuss her grand-mother's affair with Georgia and Wanetta, Penny didn't have the same reserve with her friends. The four women trusted each other. They'd always kept each other's confidences.

"There's no assuming as far as I'm concerned," Kelly said. "The man looked smart to me, and he had a *very* nice set of eyes in his head—nice butt, too—."

"Careful, Kelly, you're married."

"Married but not dead. Tell me you don't look," she challenged Pam and Janelle. "And tell me Nathan didn't see plain as day that Penny was in *love* with someone else. Any smart man would bow out grace-fully." Before Penny could voice a protest, Kelly had her hands up as though in surrender. "I know, I know. Backing off. Somebody change the subject."

Pam was happy to oblige. "How about that wild ride Penny and Joe went on to catch Ty Mason's kid. Don't you know the mayor's dying to get his hands on one of those computer gadgets."

"How in the world are you all privy to cop stuff?" Penny asked, feeling a bit bemused. "Does one of you sit on the city council or something?"

"Think about it," Pam said. "People just gotta talk. It's the law in Darby. And girls just gotta have fun, which you seem to do a lot of with your cool job and such cool gadgets."

They all laughed at Pam's sense of drama.

Then suddenly a look of horror swept over Ja-nelle's face. Her hands automatically moved to cradle her pregnant stomach as her complexion turned ashen.

Used to switching into immediate crisis mode at the drop of a pin, Penny did just that. Janelle was staring at a point over Penny's shoulder as though the diabolic specter from her worst nightmare had appeared.

And he had.

"Hello, Janelle." The voice was brutally soft and chillingly familiar.

In a matter of seconds, seconds where the entire room seemed to go into an eerie freeze-frame, Penny was out of her chair and had Don Gilard pinned to the ground, the barrel of her thirty-eight jammed against the underneath of his jaw, her forearm pressed solidly across his windpipe. The gun in his hand skittered across the gray linoleum, spinning to a stop beneath a salon chair.

After a moment of stunned confusion, his eyes began to bulge, spitting hatred and pain...and panic.

"Hurt?" she whispered, her smile feral. "Having a little trouble breathing?" She knew his right arm was broken. She'd heard it snap when she'd slammed him against the floor. His other arm was pinned with her knee.

Just a tiny bit more pressure on his windpipe and she could crush it.

"Turns out this isn't your lucky day, Donnie boy," Penny said. "You're in violation of a restraining order. That means you go straight back to jail, do not pass 'go' or collect two hundred dollars." She'd always wanted to use that Monopoly line on somebody.

She pitched her voice louder. "Somebody want to call the law and see if they can make it here before bully-boy runs out of air? It appears my hands are full and I just don't seem to have the leverage to get my arm up off his windpipe.''

"The law's already here," Joe said from above her. There was steel in his voice. And amusement.

"You didn't waste any time getting here."

"I try to be prompt. Need a hand up, 007?"

"Do you insist?"

"'Fraid so.''

"I guess you've got a bit of luck after all, Gilard. Though I'm really unhappy that you screwed up my manicure. Again.'' Without assistance, Penny stood, keeping her gun trained on the piece of scum who'd once taken drunken fists to her friend.

"Up you go, Gilard.'' Joe reached down and gripped Don's arm to bring him to his feet. Don screamed in pain and Joe frowned, looking at Penny for enlightenment.

She shrugged, kept a bland expression on her face. "Broken arm, I think.''

"Imagine that.'' They were both thinking that it served him right. Five years ago, Don Gilard had broken his wife's arm in an unprovoked rage. Kelly had relayed the details to Penny in a letter. Joe had seen it firsthand.

Once the other officers had taken Gilard into custody, Penny lowered her gun and looked around. Kelly and Pam had Janelle in the corner of the room trying to shield her from the worst of the melee.

As her gaze automatically scanned the room, she noticed a man standing in the background. She didn't recognize him. But she recognized the type, the stance. Mitchell had obviously sent the locator even though she hadn't called back and given the go-ahead.

Joe saw the direction of her gaze. He gestured with his head. "One of your guys. He was tailing Gilard, called and gave me a head's up."

"So that's how you showed up in the nick of time. I was about to accuse you of following me."

Joe grinned. "I love to follow you, Archer. That backside's a feast for the eyes."

Penny blushed. "Get out of here, Colter. Go book your felon and get him sent back where he belongs." Her words were light but she was starting to shake, the adrenaline rush subsiding.

She should have known Joe would notice. He didn't seem to miss a thing.

"Do you want to sit?" He rested his hand at the back of her neck and for just a moment she let herself lean against him while he massaged her tense muscles.

"I'm okay. Thanks for getting here so quick."

"Thank you for doing my job. Did I mention that I'm proud of your restraint in not shooting him?"

Penny smiled into his shirtfront, then straightened and stood on her own. They were putting on a show in public. "I should get a medal."

"And I should get an EKG. You're tough on a man's heart, Archer. In more ways than one." He kissed her forehead, brushed his knuckles over her cheek. "I know you'll want to be with Janelle for a bit. As soon as you can, come to the station so we can get the paperwork done."

She nodded and went to the huddle of her friends.

''Did someone call Janelle's husband?''

''I did,'' Pam said. ''He's on his way.''

When Janelle's terror-stricken eyes started to follow Don's progress out the door, Penny cupped her friend's cheeks, turned her face away.

''Don't look at him, Janelle. He's scum and he doesn't deserve a second of your recognition. It's over now, sweetie, and you're safe.''

As though a light had suddenly been switched on, Janelle's eyes cleared. She looked at Penny and all her innate compassion and sweetness poured out. She hugged Penny to her.

''Oh, Penny, you're priceless. You stand here in your sexy clothes and dynamite body, then turn into a lethal weapon and impress the hell out of me by getting in a brawl in my beauty shop, and then you call me sweetie!''

Penny pulled back and grinned at Janelle. ''And I don't recall *you* ever saying hell before.'' So much for worrying over her friend falling apart. Oh, there would be emotions to deal with for a little while now, but Janelle wouldn't slide back into the shell she'd once been in.

''I've never seen anything like that—outside of television,'' Pam said.

''No big deal.''

''Yes,'' Janelle said softly. ''It's a very big deal.''

''Thank goodness my boys weren't here,'' Kelly said, attempting to lighten the pall of horror they all felt. ''I'd have never heard the end of it.''

JOE KNEW the exact moment that Penny came through the doors of the police station. He couldn't see her yet, but he heard the buzz, a slight shift in atmosphere, as though everyone had come to attention.

He felt a smile tug at his lips. Penny Archer definitely inspired awe—although she'd taken a good ten years off his life by body slamming Gilard the way she had. He'd seen the whole thing unfold right through the window of the beauty shop and his heart had nearly stopped.

It was difficult to get used to seeing Penny with a gun in her hand, using her athletic abilities, utilizing high-tech gizmos on her computer.

Because she intrigued him—and because she was so close-mouthed about her life these past years, he'd done a simple background check on her. He hadn't intended to. A few taps on the computer keys and he'd found himself typing in Penny's name.

He'd been stunned to find no trace of her. It was as though she didn't exist—had *never* existed.

Yet, he knew she did. Because he was looking at her right now where she'd paused by dispatch to talk with Karen. Two of his officers were also watching her—both men with huge cases of hero worship.

Well, hell. Why wouldn't they want to worship the ground she walked on? She had a body that wouldn't quit, displayed very nicely in a pair of skintight jeans, and a little shirt that looked like it had been shrink-wrapped to her body. The clothes were the woman and the woman was the clothes. And the package was stunning. Add in her mysterious aura and her skills and there weren't words to describe her.

Whatever work she actually did had to be highly

classified, and most likely dangerous, if someone had gone to the trouble to remove her identity from every computer data bank he'd known to access.

He started to stand, intending to rescue her from Karen's endless questions, but at that moment, she turned, met his gaze.

His heart actually thumped behind his breastbone. A pure shot of adrenaline turned his knees to jelly, much the same feeling as facing the business end of a gun in a dark alley.

He'd never realized how closely fear and desire were linked.

She came forward, didn't speak, stopped in front of his desk and looked down at him.

And every coherent, logical thought swept right out of his brain.

"It must be hell trying to get credit-card approval."

Her full lips slowly tilted and her eyes twinkled. "Been doing a little checking up on me, Chief?"

Her tone let him know she wasn't annoyed, and he relaxed a bit, tried to act as nonchalant as she was. It was difficult when his heart was racing and he wanted nothing more than to come around the desk and kiss those sassy lips until she didn't even remember her name. Until she was as confused and needy and tied in knots as he was.

Instead, he motioned to the chair in front of his desk. "A little." Taking his cue from her, he pretended it was no big deal. But it was a big deal. What did he really have to offer this woman? How could he ever compete with her career?

"Hey," she said, reaching across the desk and giving his hand a nudge. "No sense to look all mad and macho. If it makes you feel any better, I pulled up your files, too."

His tension softened. "Bet you found more than I did."

"Bet I did." She smiled like the cat that ate the bird. "So, did you get our bully locked up nice and tight?"

"Yes. It's hard to get used to what he's turned into. Who would have ever thought this of him in school? He was on the debate team, for God's sake."

"You just never know what's in a person's genes," Penny said, feeling a jolt of sadness that cut her right to the quick. She saw that Joe was watching her and deliberately gave him an easy smile. "Have you determined if he has an alibi for the night the records hall was broken into?"

"Yes. Airtight. He was with his parole officer. He skipped right after that."

"So, one suspect down. How about the kids?"

"They're not talking."

Penny sighed. She hadn't thought Don Gilard had been the one inside her house. But because of his background, they would suspect him of causing so much as a chip on the sidewalk.

"Speaking of talking, who do you want me to give my statement to?"

"Darren was the actual arresting officer, so he has the paperwork."

Penny stood. "Then I'll get to it so we can get home."

So we can get home. The words seemed to echo between them.

They were thrown together by circumstances and an unsolved mystery that seemed to revolve around her and her grandmother's house. And though they'd taken the relationship a step further into intimacy, Penny was very careful to avoid any references to a future.

The times when she looked at Joe and desperately, *desperately* wanted more, invariably something would jolt her back to reality…

Like her inadvertent reference to Don Gilard's uncertain genes.

A reminder that Penny's as well were unsound.

PENNY HAD just finished giving the last of the details to Darren for his report when the front door swung open. A tall man, thick around the middle and just starting to go bald breezed in, bringing with him an air of authority.

"Commotion," he mumbled. "Every time I turn around there's a commotion." He stopped dead in his tracks when he saw Penny.

"Agnes Archer's granddaughter, right?" He came forward, holding out his hand. "Mayor Ben Upton. I heard how you used that high-tech computer of yours and helped apprehend Ty Mason's boys. Not that they're hardened criminals or anything, but of course you and Joe didn't know that at the time, did you?"

Several times Penny opened her mouth to speak, only to shut it again when the Mayor plowed forward.

She glanced around, saw Joe coming to her rescue.

Well, he was being awfully slow about it. And he was grinning like a hyena.

"Joe, my boy." Upton's voice boomed and ever the politician, he held out his hand in greeting. "I've just been acquainting myself with our hometown legend."

"Now, Mayor…" Penny began, then simply gave in gracefully when he steamrollered right over her words.

"Sorry, didn't mean to embarrass you. But you're just about the biggest celebrity we've had in Darby."

"I'm not a celebrity, Mayor Upton—"

"Call me Ben."

"Ben, then." Why did everyone insist on putting her on this pedestal? "I merely work for a branch of our government."

"And our government is very lucky to have you, the way I hear it. I'd like to get a look at that computer gizmo you used the other day. Heat sensor using satellites. You know, I've been saying we need to update our equipment here in Darby. Now, in light of the crime wave, I'm absolutely thinking that's what we need to do."

They were hardly having a crime wave, but Penny didn't dare interrupt.

"Perhaps you'd consider doing some outside consulting for us? Help us bring this department up-to-date. We'd have to get the council to let go of some money, but I'm certain I can persuade them. What do you think?"

Penny tucked her hair behind her ear and stood up.

"I'm afraid by the time the city council approved the expenditure and ordered the equipment, I'll be gone."

"You're not staying, then. I thought..." His words trailed off as he looked from Penny to Joe and back again. "Well, the city of Darby is grateful for your assistance to our police department. And...well, you just keep that job offer in mind, hmm?" He shook hands again with both Penny and Joe, then left in the same boisterous manner as he'd come in, greeting everyone he passed.

Joe watched Penny struggle with the attention she was receiving, and with the obvious reference to them as a couple. By now, it was all over town that Joe Colter was seeing Penny Archer.

Living with her. Never mind that they'd entered into the arrangement for her protection—at least that's what he told himself.

He moved up beside her. "Ready to go?"

She nodded. "If Darren's done with me."

"All done," Darren said. "Thanks for your cooperation. I wish all my witnesses were as thorough and had your kind of immediate recall."

As they walked out of the station, Joe couldn't help noticing the eyes following them. Following Penny, rather. It made him feel about ten feet tall that he was the man with his arm around her.

He slid his palm to the back of her neck and massaged, the heavy mass of her curly hair resting against the back of his hand.

"Mmm," she murmured. "Can we stop a minute so I can fully appreciate this?"

"I give a great full-body massage."

"Since I've never had one, I wouldn't know a good one from a bad one, but from where I'm standing, you're off to a fabulous start."

"You're kidding? You're never had a massage?"

"No."

"You're in for a big treat, then. It'll be my extreme pleasure to further your education when we get home."

"I might just hold you to that." She rotated her shoulder. "This is turning into a dangerous town."

She said it teasingly, but there was more truth there than Joe was comfortable with.

"Then I guess the town better watch out. You are one impressive, dangerous lady."

"Thanks to you."

"Me?" He pulled her to a halt beside her car, turned her to face him.

"Mmm. I was so angry that you'd only gone out with me on a bet...as long as you don't let this go to your head, I'll admit that I was still smarting three years later when I went to work for Mitchell Forbes. He made me take self-defense lessons and weapons instruction. It was sort of an anger management, healing thing. I excelled at both sports."

He put his arms around her, held her, uncaring that they were out on Main Street in twilight. "I'm so sorry about that bet."

"Water under the bridge, Colter."

He gazed down at her. "I'd rather cut off my arm than hurt you."

Penny pulled back and dug in her purse for her car keys. This was getting way too serious. If it went on much longer, she was going to do something stupid. Either bawl like a baby or blurt out her feelings.

"Your apology was just fine, Chief. No need to cut off body parts."

He shook his head and sighed. "We were doing so good. You've raised your shield again."

"What do you mean? I'm not raising any shields."

"You call me chief when you're backing away from me."

"You call me 007," she said in defense.

"But *I'm* not backing away," he said gently and put his hand on her shoulder, stopping her from getting in the car. "I call you 007 when I'm amused or impressed or so damned intrigued with you, I want to shout it to the town."

"Joe…"

"It's how I feel, Penny."

He came as close to saying the words as he could without actually uttering them. And Penny was grateful that he didn't.

As long as he didn't put voice to those three words, she could pretend that they weren't hurting each other, that they were merely intimate friends who could laugh and love and part with a kiss on the cheek and a fond farewell.

Yeah, sure.

Chapter Eleven

Penny stood in the kitchen doorway, gazing into the living room. "I really should get the rest of this stuff in boxes. I still have the basement to tackle."

Joe came up behind her, wrapped his arms around her waist, and walked her forward into the room. "Uh-uh. You've had enough exertion for one day. Besides, I promised you a massage."

She glanced over her shoulder at him, giggled when their feet nearly tangled. She loved the way his arms felt around her, the way he seemed to surround her. "I was kidding about that. I'm fine, really."

"I wasn't kidding." He urged her down on a narrow bench upholstered in celery brocade that was fraying and in bad need of repair. "Stay right here. Don't move a muscle."

He didn't have to ask twice. Her muscles didn't feel much like moving anyway. He came back into the room a few minutes later carrying a towel and her bottle of sesame oil she kept in the shower.

"What in the world?"

He straddled the bench and shifted her to do the same, her back to him. "Tools of the trade."

"Massage isn't your trade. And you're not pouring oil on me."

"Would you just relax and let me drive for once?"

That made her smile. It was so fun to try and get the better of him. Their one-upmanship game was just that. A fun, friendly game.

"Okay, Colter. But let's keep it clinical, okay? I've got a lot of stuff to do tonight."

His brows climbed. That wicked spark in his hazel eyes made her nervous, but the instant his fingers touched her neck, her resistance melted. He really did have great hands.

The smell of sesame wafted around her and Penny slumped forward, nearly purring as his thumbs worked pressure points in her neck, then firmly skimmed up and down her arms.

"That feels great."

"It'd probably feel better if you'd lie down."

"Said the spider to the fly," she mumbled.

Joe laughed. "This settee thing is plenty wide enough for you to stretch out on."

"Clinical, Joe, remember?"

"Have you ever had a *clinical* massage where you were sitting up?"

"I told you. I've never had a massage, period."

"Well, then, you have no basis for comparison. How do you know I'm not doing it *clinically?*"

She felt her lips twitch. "Because I'm feeling restless rather than relaxed."

He chuckled and slipped the strap of her tank top off her shoulder.

"Joe…"

"Relax." His fingers kneaded and stroked. Flames of sensation licked at her nerve endings. "Sure you don't want to take off your top?" he asked.

"No."

"No, you're not sure, or no you don't want to take it off?"

He shifted on the settee behind her, his legs cradling her in a sensual vise. His palms stroked down her arms then settled on her waist, burrowing under her tank top, inching it up as his thumbs circled each disk of her vertebrae, traveling upward. The brush of his fingertips against the sides of her breasts nearly jolted her off the bench. She didn't know how much more she could take.

"Are you trying to seduce me, Joe?"

"Yeah, I am. Is it working?"

Penny knew they shouldn't keep on this way. Joe had some misguided notion of protecting her. But that wouldn't be forever. She should really be pulling back from him rather than letting him get closer. Letting him make her feel special, cherished.

But besides making her feel special, he made her feel like a woman. She wanted to explore the femininity he brought out in her, test it, share it, revel in it.

She felt like a candle and Joe was her flame. Just a simple touch and she'd ignite.

The slight pressure of his fingers, motionless now against the sides of her breasts, made her dizzy, needy, expectant. She had two choices—turn into him, or run like hell.

Oh, God, she wanted to ignite. She'd never wanted something so bad in her life.

To hell with the packing, she thought. To hell with creating distance.

"Penny?" His warm breath caressed her cheek, sending sparks of longing straight through her.

Urgency swamped her as she twisted on the bench and whipped her shirt over her head. "Yes, by damn," she breathed. "It's working."

He didn't need any more urging. He grasped the backs of her thighs and pulled her onto his lap so that she was straddling him. Her breasts nestled against his bare chest as she pressed into him, fusing her mouth with his in a frenzy of pent-up desire that left her reeling.

His kiss was like a fine, expensive wine, liquid and tranquilizing, yet stimulating beyond belief...beyond any that they'd shared before. Each time, each kiss was so new. So different. So perfect.

He ran his tongue over her neck, then back to her mouth. She tasted her own perfume on his lips.

He reached for the bottle of oil he'd set on the floor. Holding her gaze with his, he dribbled sesame-scented liquid down her chest, then slowly began to spread it. She moaned and arched her body, positive she'd never experienced anything this erotic and decadent. Warm oil trickled down the front of her body, soaking into the waistband of her jeans.

His large, warm hands circled her breasts, stroking, worshipping, coming close, but never quite touching her nipples.

It was exquisite torture, pure and simple.

Penny gripped his wrists and guided his hands to the center of her breasts. Slick oil oozed through her fingers, coating her palms.

"Something wrong?" His steady, heated gaze held her, watching...inflaming. She should have felt embarrassed by his scrutiny, by her own urgency and boldness. Instead, she felt empowered and so sensitized she feared she might shatter.

"You're teasing me...and driving me wild."

"Then I'm on the right track." His fingers plucked at her nipples. She felt as if an invisible string was being tugged, a string that went straight to the core of her desire. She transferred her hands to his chest, rubbing, stroking, arousing, reveling in the sharp catch of his breath.

Anticipation throbbed in every pulse point. She squirmed in his lap, rocking against him, frustrated with the barrier of denim between them.

"I need to feel you."

He stood, keeping one arm around her waist, lifting her. With his free hand, he unsnapped her jeans and pushed them over her hips until they fell to the floor. His strength thrilled her, and surprised her. He made her feel petite, as though he could just lift her up and tote her around like a doll.

Feeling more aroused than she thought possible, she jerked at his clothing, using her hands and feet, sacrificing adroitness for speed. When awkwardness became a hindrance, he set her on the floor long enough to finish undressing, then lifted her back in his arms, pressing his mouth to her neck, and then to her lips with a feverish desire that left her stunned.

She wrapped her legs around his waist, sucked in a breath when the hard length of him pressed against her. His slick hands stroked her, his fingers searching, touching, opening her for exploration.

When his fingers delved into her, Penny cried out and came to an immediate, earth shattering orgasm. He didn't give her a chance to come down. Instead, he renewed his sensual exploration, bringing her right back up to the peak, slowing down just before she toppled over the edge again.

She nearly sobbed as need and tension swept her.

"Joe!" she cried, squirming against him. Her hands touched every inch of him that she could reach. She couldn't get enough of him. She wanted more. Much more. "Please."

He sat back on the bench, holding her straddled over his lap, guiding her. Her blood smoldered as she lowered herself onto him, feeling him with every cell of her body; the hair-roughened thighs beneath her own, the strength of his palms cupping her hips, the carnal friction as the tips of her breasts brushed his chest. For an instant, neither one moved, caught up in the thrilling, erotic, ecstatic feel of their bodies joined in deep penetration.

"I've always remembered you just like this," he whispered.

"How?"

"Strong and sexy and sweet."

"I'm not feeling especially sweet right now." Her breath came in short, hungry pants. Need overwhelmed her, demanding that she reach for it, take pleasure and give it back in kind. She felt him throb inside her, drenching her in sensuality.

"No? Probably this bench thing we're sitting on. There are some definite possibilities if you're into acting out fantasies."

"Mmm," Penny murmured, giving an experimental wiggle. When Joe sucked in a breath, she smiled. She liked this power she held over him, the power to make him weak. She nibbled at the corner of his lips, then traced them with her tongue.

"Definite possibilities. You want to stop and talk about them?" She rocked against him and his fingers flexed on her behind.

"No way. Next time, though."

"Deal." The powerful feelings had reached a boiling point and were about to explode. Penny could no longer deny them. "I'm ready, Joe," she said, panting.

He started to shift their positions, but Penny shook her head. "No. I'm in the driver's seat on this trip."

"I'm only an inch away from losing it, baby." His teeth were gritted, sweat dripped from his temples.

"Then let's take it over the top." She didn't think about decorum or finesse or the fact that she rarely acted this bold. All she thought about was that she wanted it faster, hotter, higher. She arched back, closing her eyes, her movements fast and agile. Then she opened her eyes and locked her gaze with Joe's.

One expertly executed move brought them to immediate flash point. And that's when any thoughts of expertise gave way to sheer spiraling ecstasy. With what little breath she could gather, she cried out, and then simply held on as wave after wave of exquisite pleasure clutched her body and blanked her mind.

Exhausted, Penny collapsed against Joe. Slick oil mingled with sweat, causing her breasts to slip erotically against his chest. If it weren't for his tight hold around her waist, she'd have probably slid right off his lap.

"There's something to be said about an athletic woman," Joe commented when he'd recovered his breath.

Penny didn't know whether to be embarrassed or elated. She leaned back and gave him a sassy smile. "And what might that be?"

"Hot. Incredible. Better than my fantasies."

She ran her palms over his slick shoulders, down his breastbone, circling the muscled swell of his chest, grazing his nipples. "I probably wouldn't object if you wanted to tell me those fantasies now."

He sucked in a breath, his hands tightening around her hips. "What happened to the burning need to pack?"

"Something else is burning hotter."

He grinned. "Give me a couple minutes to recuperate. I think you've worn me out."

Penny feigned shock and deliberately pressed against him. "Are you actually admitting I'm in better shape than you are?"

He pressed his lips to the side of her neck. "What will it get me if I do?"

"What do you want it to get you?" She meant the question in jest.

"You. All of you."

She pressed her lips together, sighed. "Joe…"

"I know. You're leaving."

She nodded. "Can't we just enjoy what we have right now?"

"I want more, Penny." His voice was soft, raw with emotions.

She wrapped her arms around his neck, pressed against him, held on tight. "I know."

Just that. What more could she say? Joe had a ranch that represented his dream. He needed roots and family. Here in Darby.

Penny had a job waiting for her in west Texas, a chance to be all that she'd ever wanted to be.

If she could be the woman that Joe needed, give him babies, she might be willing to give up her goal of being an agent. But she wasn't that woman. And staying much longer was only going to make their parting worse.

It was almost July. Her training started on the fifteenth. Just the thought of being without him made a lump form in her throat.

"Take me to bed, Joe. I want to shut out the night. And the world."

"We can't run forever."

"Maybe not forever. But we can run tonight."

THE LIGHT on her message machine was blinking the next morning when Penny stumbled out of her bedroom in search of coffee.

Debating, she went for coffee first. She'd gotten very little sleep last night, had lost count of how many times they'd made love. Joe had already called in and taken the day off, claiming since he'd sidetracked her with the massage, it was his duty to help her clean out the attic and basement.

With this insatiable need clawing at both of them, she had to wonder how much work they'd get done. And if they'd survive.

After she'd poured herself a cup of coffee and one to take back to bed for Joe, she paused by the message machine and hit the play button.

''It's Pam. Call me. An offer came in on your grandmother's house.''

Penny frowned, set down the two coffee cups and dialed Pam's number.

''Pam, it's Penny. How can you have an offer on the house? We haven't even officially listed it yet.''

''I know. But he came to me. And you are planning to sell it, right?''

''Yes, but you haven't even showed it.''

''He said he'd seen it. He's offering over market value with a stipulation that the property come as is with the contents included.''

''Contents? As in my furniture?'' She saw Joe come out of the bedroom. For a moment her mind snagged. He was too sexy and handsome. Picking up a coffee cup, she held it out to him and tried to concentrate on what Pam was telling her.

''He said furniture and *everything*. He was quite specific about that.''

''Why?''

Pam's voice held a shrug. ''Something about keeping the ambiance of an old house completely intact.

He couldn't see you getting rid of stuff he'd be perfectly happy to have.''

"Who is this potential buyer?"

"I'm not supposed divulge the name of my client."

"Pam. Someone's claiming to have seen this house, but *I* haven't shown it—and since there's no lockbox, I'm ninety-nine percent certain you haven't shown it either. And he wants my grandmother's personal belongings. Despite the fact that I couldn't agree to those terms, the whole thing sounds odd.''

Joe was starting to shift beside her, looking as though he wanted to listen to the conversation along with her. She held up her finger, silently telling him she'd bring him up to speed in a minute.

"I know," Pam said. "And I said I'm not *supposed* to tell names, but in this case I'm making an exception. It's that hunky guy who's been trying to court you, the one you said left town.''

"Nathan?" Penny's voice rose and Joe's brows slammed down.

"What about Nathan?" he asked.

Penny held up her hand for silence. "Pam, when did you see him?"

"This morning. Called and got me out of bed. I met him at the office and wrote up the offer. You can make a counter offer on the personal belongings stipulation, Penny. Then it'll be up to him to take or leave the deal. But the guy's offering more money than the house is actually worth. And you *do* intend to sell it.''

"Yes, but…stall him, Pam."

"Oh, you're on to something, I can tell." Unholy

glee fairly sang in Pam's voice. Penny decided that Pam really *should* become a writer. Her imagination was sharp and vivid.

"I just want to check a couple of things. If he presses you, tell him it's no deal on Grandma's personal items. Tell him you think I might be on the verge of changing my mind about selling, and that you'll see what you can do to talk me around."

"Okay, I can handle that. You'll keep me posted on what you're doing, though, right?"

"Yes. You've got my cell phone number, don't you?" Penny asked.

"I've got it."

"Okay. If you need me for anything—if *anything* seems the least bit odd or makes you uncomfortable, you call me immediately."

"Are you worried about Nathan for some reason? You almost sound like he's someone to fear."

"I just want to know a little more about him, that's all."

Penny hung up, and with Joe on her heels, she headed straight for the kitchen where she'd left her laptop computer.

"What's gong on?"

"Pam got an offer on the house."

"I gathered that much. You said Nathan's name. What does he have to do with this?"

She powered up the computer, pacing. "Hc's the one who put in the offer. He wants it lock, stock and barrel. And as much as I'd like to get out of packing and sorting and dealing with all the odds and ends here, that just hits me a little wrong. That and the fact that the guy's had me alone enough times. If he wanted the house he had plenty of opportunity to say something to me about it.''

''I don't think we want to talk about Nathan having you alone.''

''Jealous, Colter?'' She grinned at him and sat down at the kitchen table, tapping the computer keys. Her fingers moved swiftly, expertly.

Joe watched over her shoulder. He only knew enough about computers to get him by—which wasn't much at all. ''You're pretty good with that thing.''

''I learned from an ace hacker.''

''One of these days you're going to tell me all about that job of yours.''

''Mmm-hmm.''

His brows rose when he saw what she'd pulled up on her screen. Even as a police officer, he didn't have access to these kind of files.

''Uh, I hate to be a stuffed shirt about all this, but is what you're doing on the up-and-up?''

Her lips twitched. ''Are you going to arrest me if I say no?''

He raked a hand through his hair and sat down.

''Relax, Joe. I'm not compromising the security of our nation or hurting anyone. I'm simply trespassing a bit.''

''I'm abetting a pirate hacker,'' he said. The scope of her abilities continued to astound him, kept him off balance.

''Oh, stop. I'm not copying anything, and it's not as though I'm transferring funds or trading on information I find. Well.''

"Well, what?" He leaned closer.

The woodsy smell of his aftershave nearly made her lose her train of thought. Impulsively, she pecked a kiss to his cheek, then turned back to the information on her screen.

"Our boy is who he says he is—pretty much. Mother is alive, he *does* have two dogs."

That kiss on the cheek stirred him up, and since he was having trouble seeing over her shoulder, Joe stood and plucked her out of the chair.

She shrieked. "Joe!"

He casually sat down with her in his lap and crossed his arms over her waist causing her silky kimono to shift against her sensitized breasts. "What do you mean, *does?*"

"He told me." Her hands lay motionless in her lap for a moment.

He grinned at her look of astonishment, the desire that made her jaw go slack. He tightened his arms, pressed her more firmly in his lap, torturing himself. "And that file corroborates that he has animals?"

Her gaze was locked onto his, as though she were in a trance, held in a sensual spell. Her voice was a breathy whisper, her brown eyes glazed with desire. "Yes."

"Do we care if he has animals?"

She swallowed, turned back to the screen, scrolled down the information. "Somebody does. Evidently the government's been keeping tabs on him. His grandfather is indeed Al Lantrelle—who six months ago was admitted to the infirmary…in *prison.*"

She shifted in his lap and Joe nearly had a heart attack.

"Good old Granddaddy was connected to a gold heist at a small refinery in the late seventies. They couldn't get the goods on him, but busted him for another bank robbery a few weeks later. He's been in prison twenty years."

"And Nathan?"

She scrolled down the page. "He stole a six-pack of beer at seventeen. A parking ticket that went to warrant. Nothing federal."

"Yet there's a federal file on him."

"Begs a few questions, doesn't it?"

"Like why the sudden need to meet your grandmother. Then make an offer on the house."

"You don't suppose..." Penny looked around.

"That we're sitting on a gold mine?"

"It's possible. Joe, I remember a man when I was about fourteen years old. My dad wasn't around when the guy came into town. It was just Grandmother and me. And for a few days she glowed like a girl in springtime. It was astonishing. I saw a side to her that I'd never seen. She was this beautiful, carefree...*girl*. And then he disappeared, and Grandmother became even more bitter than she'd been before." That's when her grandmother had really begun her campaign to convince Penny that men were no-good scoundrels who could never be trusted.

And perhaps that's why Penny hadn't given Joe a chance to explain about the bet all those years ago.

"Seems to me someone needs to have a chat with Lantrelle."

"Yes, and I intend to do that right away."

His hand tightened over her thigh, held her in place on his lap. "Not you, 007. You're in my jurisdiction now, and I'll do the investigating."

She was so astonished by his high-handed tone she actually gaped at him. "If you think you can stop me—"

In one smooth move, he shifted her on his lap so that her legs were hanging over the side of his legs rather than in front. Holding her still, he ran his hand up the inside of her thigh, all the way to the top, and cupped her through the silk of her panties.

She gasped, and automatically pressed against his hand. Their night of lovemaking had left her so sensitive all it took was a brush of his fingertips to have her aching all over again. "You're not playing fair, Colter."

"I'm learning."

"Learning what?"

"That it doesn't pay to play fair with you." His fingers stroked her and she moaned, curled right into him.

"I'm going to find Lantrelle and talk to him myself, Chief. But I think we've got some business in the bedroom first."

He stood with her in his arms. "Yeah. We've got business. But you keep up this talk about messing in my jurisdiction and I'll handcuff you to that bed."

She cupped her hand around the back of his neck and pulled his head down to hers, trusting that he wouldn't trip over something and dump them both on the ground.

A breath away from his lips, she tisked. "I'd be careful if I were you. You've come out on the losing end of the challenge a couple of times here lately."

"Is it a challenge you're looking for? Well, baby, you better hold on tight."

Chapter Twelve

Three hours later, they called the argument a draw and compromised, both of them going to speak with Nathan.

Joe stopped his truck outside of the motel Penny had suggested Nathan try. It was a long shot, but he didn't seem to be anywhere in town.

"You know, we might be barking up the wrong tree, reading more into something than is there."

Joe gave her a look as though she were daft.

"Well, think about it. He came to town, and he could have legitimately been tracking Grandmother down. His grandfather could have been truly sorry for hurting her. And maybe Nathan has a yen to change his surroundings. He said he liked Darby." The more she talked, the more ridiculous she sounded.

"Skeptic," she said when he still looked at her with that cocky brow raised. "And I told you we should have brought my car. He'd recognize my car and if he wants me, he'll open the door."

"Oh, he wants you," Joe said, his jaw tightening. "But he's not going to get you."

Penny looked out the window. A stinging pain

zinged through her and there was no good reason for it. She didn't want Nathan, had absolutely no feelings for him, but it still smarted that he'd sought her out—not for herself, but for another reason—the same way a high school boy had once dated the brainy girl on a bet.

Determined not to get caught up in parallels to the past, Penny checked the clip in her weapon.

Joe frowned.

"What?" she asked, nearly snapping.

He raised his brows, adjusted the sand-colored Stetson on his head. "Just noticing how easy and familiar you are with a firearm."

"I've been around them most of my life. I'll make a good partner, Joe."

"Oh, I know you will."

She'd meant as his backup. He obviously meant something entirely different.

Penny pushed open the door and hopped out of the truck, waiting as Joe came around the hood. They went in and talked with the manager, but Penny knew Nathan wasn't here. His rental car wasn't in the parking lot. Nor were any other cars.

The manager confirmed her belief and after checking the books said that Lantrelle had never been a registered guest.

Joe went over the entries himself. "Thanks, Bob. Give me a call if anyone by that name, or any outsiders for that matter show up."

"Will do, Chief."

ALTHOUGH PENNY had already done her own check on Nathan, she wasn't satisfied. She was good on a computer, but Kendra was the best. Besides, at the ranch, they had better access to information than Penny did.

Rather than spinning her wheels trying to accomplish household chores when her mind was elsewhere, she went into the kitchen and dialed the private line at Texas Confidential headquarters.

When the telephone engaged at the ranch, Penny could tell that there was a little bit of a scuffle over who was answering.

Rafe Alvarez obviously won out because his sexy, smooth-as-glass voice sounded over the line. "Hey, babe, what's shakin'?" he asked.

Penny shook her head and grinned. "*You* will be if you don't quit calling me babe—especially since I imagine your wife is sitting right next to you."

Rafe laughed. "Ah, Penny. I thought you were the only woman who could scare me. But my Kendra *does* make me shake."

Penny felt a pang of envy. The love in Rafe's voice for his wife was so clear. She sometimes imagined she heard that same note in Joe's voice. But she couldn't accept it. She shook away the thoughts.

"How is everyone?"

"Good. Chaotic. Going from a predominately male ranch to four of us getting married and all these babies underfoot is taxing Mitchell something fierce." There was a smile in Rafe's voice. "He's trying to hang tough, but he's a big old marshmallow. Back to you, now. Mitchell says you don't want us to come to Darby. We're not in agreement, Penny. Hell,

Brady, Jake, Cody and I've nearly come to blows arguing over whose qualifications are better suited to your mystery.''

Penny tisked, tried to downplay the whole thing. ''I leave for three weeks and y'all are already out of line. I thought Kendra was keeping the peace in my absence.''

''Hell, Penny, Kendra's right in the middle of the fray, claiming *she* ought to come to you.''

Tears stung Penny's eyes. These people were her family. The agents and Mitchell mainly. She hadn't had a lot of time with Catherine or Abby or Kendra and Sarah, but she didn't need time to know that they were special, to feel that they, too, were family.

''Speaking of Kendra, I did a little bit of digging on a man named Nathan Lantrelle, but I'd like Kendra to see what she can find.''

''Someone you're interested in? You want him checked out to see if he's cool to date?''

''No. We only had dinner…''

''Well, if people are breaking in and jumping you, don't go out again until we get the lowdown on him.''

''Yes, Daddy.''

Rafe gave a rich laugh. ''Should have known better than try to give you an order. I'm going to be one, by the way.''

''A father? Rafe! How wonderful for you both! Now give the phone to your wife so I can congratulate her and engage her expertise.''

After Penny spoke with Kendra, she put down the phone and just stood there, feeling her heart hang heavy in her chest. The biological clock that had been keeping her up at nights since she'd returned to Darby ticked even louder now with Rafe and Kendra's news of impending parenthood.

But there would be no kids for Penny.

All the more reason she needed to figure out who the heck was messing with her and then get out of town and get on with her life so Joe could get on with his.

So he could find a woman who could give him the family he wanted so badly.

The back screen door slapped against the frame and Joe came in muttering. "The town's hot and heavy into the Fourth of July festival and it makes me nervous. We just don't need crowds right now—" He stopped, looked up at her, really looked at her. "What is it?" He was across the room and in front of her in two strides, his gaze going from her face to the phone and back. "Did you get another call?"

"No. I called Kendra." Penny made herself smile. Obviously he was picking up on her sadness. She didn't need questions in that direction. "She's going to check further into Nathan's files, snoop in areas I can't get into."

"She must be pretty good. You got in some highly classified places."

"It's amazing how much information is out there— on each of us."

"Speaking of information, I talked to Rochelle over in county records. She finally tracked down the files that were taken in the break-in."

"And?"

"They were the architectural blueprints to this house."

Penny frowned, combed her fingers through her hair. "What next? I feel like a sitting duck. There's simply no reason for someone to target me or my grandmother like this." She sighed, feeling bone-tired. "Maybe we're just making too much out of the whole thing. Some money's come up missing, some gasoline. Stuff like that happens all the time. It doesn't necessarily mean I'm the target."

He put a hand on her shoulder, let it slip down her arm to link their fingers together. "The blueprints paint a different picture, Pen. You know that."

"I just hate this waiting stuff. Why? What does he want?"

"You're assuming Lantrelle?"

"He's the obvious suspect."

"Well, you're not waiting alone." He rested his forehead against hers. "I hate this, too. So, let's think about something else. Did you know there's an automatic garage door opener on the shelf out there?"

"Yes. I bought it and had it shipped to Grandmother about five years ago, along with the money to have it installed." She shrugged. "I guess she didn't like the gift."

He pressed his lips to her brow. "I can put it in if you like. It'd be a selling point for the house, and make it a lot easier on you rather than wrestling the heavy door by hand and locking it with the padlock."

"What's the use? I'm not going to be here much longer to wrestle with it." She suddenly wanted to cry and there was no good reason for it. She simply wanted to put her arms around Joe, hold on tight and never let go.

But she would have to let go. Soon.

He lifted her hair off her shoulders, linked his fingers together behind her neck. "You're overwhelmed, Penny."

"Get real. I don't *get* overwhelmed." Her tone was filled with affront. And weariness.

"What you need is a warm relaxing bath."

Penny's heart skipped a beat.

"You think since you're a tough girl, people wouldn't recognize your need for frills and feminine indulgence?"

She shrugged. "I guess most people don't know that about me."

"Most people don't know what you wear under these clothes…aside from that corset you wore the other day. Pretty daring to wear the underwear as outerwear."

"I found it at Wanetta's shop and couldn't resist."

"Were you able to resist the hats?"

Penny's lips twitched. "No."

"So, maybe I'll pamper you a bit, draw you a bath, help you relax and take your mind off everything else for a while. And then just maybe you'll model that sexy corset for me?"

"The corset and what else?"

"Surprise me."

PENNY HAD NEVER deliberately dressed sexily for a man, never thought she'd be bold enough to saunter into a bedroom wearing a corset and G-string underwear and nothing else except perfumed skin.

Joe was standing by the mantel in the bedroom, watching the bathroom door. Waiting for her.

She felt her skin flush, and it wasn't from the steam of the bathroom.

He went utterly still, then slowly, excruciatingly slowly, he straightened away from the fireplace mantel. The room was hushed with expectancy and sexual tension. Penny felt a fine trembling skim just beneath the surface of her skin.

An uncanny sense of unease mingled with the sensuality in the room, intruding on the moment. She felt as though everything in her life was about to come to a head.

Was it fear she felt now as she looked at Joe? What if this was their last day together? Would it ever be enough? Would a lifetime be enough?

"I am without words," he said softly, his voice rasping deep in his throat. He took a step closer, then another.

Penny stood where she was, waited. She'd never seen such an utter look of worship on a man's face. It gave her strength. It gave her confidence.

It fueled her love to overflowing.

If anything happened to Joe because of her, she'd never be able to live with the guilt and pain.

When he came within touching distance, she cupped his face in her hands and drew him down to her, kissing him with a tenderness and banked emotion that came very close to moving her to tears.

Joe skimmed his hands over her bare shoulders,

along the smooth, exposed skin of her upper back. There was a hint of quiet desperation in the way her lips clung and lingered and it made his heart pump.

He combed his fingers through her hair, pushed back the curly strands that brushed her cheeks, carefully pulled out the pins that held the heavy tresses off her neck. Her eyes were liquid brown as she looked up at him.

He could get lost in those eyes. Wanted to spend a lifetime just there.

"I love you," he said quietly.

Her eyes closed as though an ache too heavy to bear had weighed down on them. When she opened her eyes, they were wet.

He ran his thumb beneath her lower lashes. He wouldn't apologize for his feelings, nor take back the words. He didn't expect her to say them back to him. But he needed to tell her how he felt.

With a reverence he didn't even try to hide, he flattened his palms on her collarbone, smoothed them down her chest, circled the swell of her breasts where they blossomed out over the top of the Bordeaux-colored corset.

He mapped her body over the sexy, old-fashioned garment, feeling lace and satin and whalebones run beneath his palms. So many textures. Just like Penny. She was a woman of many textures and layers.

And he wanted them all.

He reached behind and unzipped the stiff satin, let it drop from her body. For just an instant, he forgot to draw a breath. She was so perfect. His every fantasy. Al he wanted in a woman—a mate.

PENNY STOOD STILL, lost in Joe's reverent gaze. She just wanted to shut the door and close the world away. For tonight.

He'd said he loved her. The reciprocal words ached in her throat, but they would remain locked there. It was best.

She wasn't the woman for him.

He undressed them both and lowered her to the bed as though she were a precious piece of china.

Her heart was breaking, but his hands and lips and body were like the greatest reward, a soothing balm that attempted to heal and keep the doom at bay, renewing her, giving, just giving. It was exquisite. It was a gift. It was everything that Penny had ever wanted and more.

And so very bittersweet because she couldn't claim nor accept what he was offering.

A tiny white pill stood between who she was and what Joe wanted. What he needed. She would take that birth control pill throughout her childbearing years.

For her, there was no other choice.

Penny didn't realize she was crying, until Joe tightened his arms around her, kissed her eyelids.

"Shh, baby." He didn't know what he was soothing. He only knew there was pain, hesitation, and sadness. He didn't want her to be sad. Love shouldn't make a person sad. But sometimes it really could hurt.

It was almost as though she was telling him goodbye. There was desperation in her touch and Joe didn't understand it.

"It'll all work out," he said.

She shook her head, but he stopped the movement with his mouth.

"Yes." Now, more than ever, he took care with her. His hands were gentler than they'd ever been, his senses so much more attuned to sensation, to each nuance of the woman beneath him.

He'd never made love like this—this quietly, this carefully, this desperately...with so much love welling inside him it made his throat ache with emotion.

With the bedroom door locked against the world and the air conditioner blowing cool air over fevered skin, they made love. Without words. Without reservations. Without hurry.

Skin whispered against skin, limbs sliding against sheets. They didn't need the words. Eyes, lips and fingertips were all that they needed for communication. Their bodies said it so much better, so much easier, so much deeper.

And through his eyes he tried to tell her it would be okay, that love would get them through, find the solutions.

THE PHONE RANG and Penny shot straight up in the bed, grabbing it on the second ring, nearly knocking a small travel alarm off the bedside table. It was 2:00 a.m.

Her voice was groggy with sleep. "Hello?"

"Hi, Penny. I'm so sorry to wake you. This is Karen from the police department. Is the chief there by any chance?"

By a very big chance, Penny thought. The whole town knew exactly where Joe Colter was staying. Oh, they probably didn't know he was right next to her in the bed, but she imagined they'd speculated over that plenty.

"It's for you. It's Karen."

He sat up, frowned at the illuminated dial of his watch. "Karen? What's up?"

"What *isn't* up? I've never seen anything like this in my twenty years in this town. Darren's out at a suspicious fire on Potoh Creek Road, Larry's handling a report of domestic violence over at the Sidney place, and I just got an anonymous tip of a possible bank robbery in progress. We're stretched thin, Joe. It's like there's a full moon or something."

"I'll be there in a few minutes, Karen."

He hung up the phone and got up to put on his clothes.

"What's wrong?" Penny asked.

"Suspicious activity at the bank." He snapped his jeans, threaded his arms through the sleeves of a T-shirt, and pulled it over his head. Not exactly chief of police attire, but then, it was the middle of the night. "The town's hopping tonight with a fire and a family going at each other. Karen's nervous."

Penny smiled. "She's not used to several calls at once?"

"No."

"Want me to come along and help?"

He shook his head. "No need. You stay here and get some sleep. I shouldn't be gone too long."

Penny snuggled down between the sheets, actually glad that it wasn't her on call. Her body was worn out, perhaps a good deal of that was because of her emotions. But she felt as though she'd been pulled through a knothole backward and could sleep for a week.

"You go on, then."

"You've got your gun?"

"Right beside me. I'm safe, Joe."

He kissed her lips, lingered for just a moment. "I'll call if I'm going to be long."

"Just don't call too early."

"Okay, sleepyhead."

She heard him let himself out the door and lock it, heard the engine of the squad car fire to life. He'd been bringing the police vehicle home, figuring it made a statement by being in her driveway.

She smiled and pulled the sheet up to her chin, started to close her eyes again. That's when she heard the key in the door.

What had he forgotten?

Knowing it would probably take a while for her to get back to sleep, she tossed off the covers and slipped on a pair of jogging shorts and a T-shirt.

Barefooted, she opened the bedroom and screamed.

"You…how did you…?"

She never had a chance to finish the question.

Chapter Thirteen

Joe was getting a really bad feeling. Not even a breeze stirred in the night air. The bank windows were dark, the alarm mechanism undisturbed.

His heart started to pound in earnest. Walking back to the car, his steps picked up, then became a run.

What the heck was going on in their peaceful town? The mayor was going to have a fit.

He started the squad car, slammed it into gear and spun the tires as he pulled a U-turn on Main Street and sped back toward the residential area, punching in Penny's phone number on his cell phone.

The telephone rang and rang. At last the machine picked up. He was reluctant to leave a message. He wasn't sure who was in the house.

Hoping his imagination was simply running away with him, that she was merely sleeping or showering and didn't hear the phone, he stabbed the end button and got on the radio, requesting back up at the Archer residence.

With the lights off on the squad car, he rounded the final corner and wheeled into the driveway, stopped about ten feet from the garage door. Releasing the safety strap on his gun, he jumped out of the car.

The collie was whining and scratching at the back door.

Movement at the rear of the house sent his adrenaline soaring.

Lantrelle. Skulking around the bushes, peering into the window.

Anger worse than any he'd ever experienced swept over him, hazed his mind. He didn't need the gun. His bare hands would do.

He hit the man in a full body check and they went down on the grass. Blind rage lent him the strength to pin Lantrelle to the ground. It took every ounce of his considerable control not to follow through on his instincts and beat the guy to a pulp.

"You're under arrest." He struggled with the man, managing to get the handcuffs off his belt and snapped onto Nathan's wrists, then hauled him to his feet.

WHEN PENNY CAME TO, her head ached and her lungs burned. Her mind was sluggish, but she forced herself to think. It was hard. Thoughts formed, then flitted away.

Where was she? The garage? But that didn't make sense...In her car?

Concentrate.

Hazy images gelled in jerky segments. Her heart thudded. He'd had a key. That's how he'd gotten into the house.

She had an idea if she were to look in her purse

she'd find that along with the missing forty dollars, her spare key she had made was also gone.

But a missing key was the least of her worries right now. Her nose and eyes burned from the carbon monoxide filling her lungs and fogging the garage.

She shut off the Cadillac's engine, stumbled out and tried to push open the garage door.

It wouldn't budge. Someone must have threaded the padlock through the latch.

Think, Penny. Splinters speared her palms. The wood on the door was rotting. Coughing, she put her arm over her nose, trying to escape the asphyxiating stench of deadly fumes. There were no windows to break, no side doors to open.

She made her way back to the car, her heart pumping. By damn, she would not die this day. Not like this.

She turned the key in the ignition, put the gear into Reverse, squeezed her hands tight around the steering wheel and stomped the gas pedal to the floor.

The Cadillac shot backward with a powerful squeal of tires and shattering wood.

Fragments of the busted garage door dented the hood and flew in every direction.

Expecting a clear driveway, her gaze darted to the rearview mirror. In the same instant that visual registered in her brain, Penny's head whipped nearly off her shoulders as she rammed into the solid front end of Joe's squad car.

She might have laughed at the stunned look on his face, the startled yelp as he leaped out of the way—

dragging another man with him—but she needed air. Fast. Desperately.

She shut off the car and stumbled out the door.

"What the hell?" Joe caught her by the shoulders, struggled to hold her still as she coughed and tried to pull away. His sluggish brain finally caught up with the events and with a sickening sense of dread, he realized what had happened.

Or almost happened.

"Baby, take it easy. Breathe. I've got you now."

His hands were shaking and he was beside himself with fear. He couldn't handle it, he decided. It suddenly came home to him that she likely went through this kind of torture and danger as a matter of course in her job. He knew his heart wouldn't be able to take it on a daily basis. Now he had a better understanding how some wives would have trouble with their husband's decisions to be in dangerous professions.

He turned back to Lantrelle, who was handcuffed and shaking beside the car.

This Ivy League preppie had tried to kill Penny, locking her in the garage in a running car.

"I'll kill you."

Before he could take a step, Penny grabbed for his shirtsleeve. "Wrong Lantrelle, Chief." Her voice rasped past the abuse her throat had taken.

"That's what I've been trying to tell you," Nathan said, out of breath. "My grandfather is in the house."

Joe went utterly still. "What?"

"He's looking for gold he hid here years ago. I knew he'd come back for it. I tried to get here ahead of him so he wouldn't do something stupid and end up in jail again.''

"How do I know the two of you aren't partners?'' As long as Penny was out here by his side, out of harm's way, he could take the time to get the story, to get the facts so he knew what he'd be walking into.

"We're not partners. You're going to have to take my word for it. He's an old man, but he's had a lot of years to think about this gold. He's not going to let anyone stop him.''

"He had a key.'' Penny wanted to lean on Joe, but knew she needed to stand on her own. This rough-and-tumble stuff was more than she'd bargained for. "But the man who mowed me down on the porch the other week didn't have the feel of an eighty-year-old,'' she said, looking at Nathan.

"That was me—and I'm sorry. I thought I could get here and get the gold and end this whole mess before it got off the ground, before Grandpa got involved.''

"You told me he'd died.''

"I know it looks bad. But I was trying to protect you. Even the offer on the house. I didn't want you hurt.''

"And the stolen blueprints?''

Nathan nodded his admission. "I needed to know the layout of the house.''

Penny wondered if someone should advise him of his rights, remind him he probably ought not to be speaking so freely without the advice of an attorney.

But a feminine prick to her ego kept her silent. This man had courted her on false pretenses. Never mind that she wasn't interested. It was the principle of the matter.

And the Lantrelle family members had caused her and her grandmother plenty of grief.

"If you'd managed to find the gold and taken it, you would have been guilty of theft. Did you think of that?"

"No. I didn't think. I'm a systems analyst, not Pretty Boy Floyd."

The gangster reference reminded her of the man in her house. Penny glanced at her smashed in trunk, then looked at Joe. "Once again, I find myself without a weapon. I don't suppose you'll give me yours?"

"Not a chance. You're going to stay put."

She shook her head. "There's an intruder in my house."

"And that house is in my jurisdiction."

She glanced over his shoulder and sighed. "Yeah, well you've got crowd control to deal with in your jurisdiction." Georgia and Wanetta were trotting spryly across the street, nightclothes flapping around their ankles, shotguns bouncing in their arms.

"There's no need for weapons," Nathan said. "Gramps is an old man. He really is dying. Let me go in and talk with him."

Penny didn't believe Nathan was as innocent as he tried to sound. She had an idea he was trying desperately to cover his tail. "That old man managed to knock me out and drag me into the garage," she pointed out.

The reminder had Joe's expression darkening like a thunderhead. "No one is going anywhere. You're all going to stand back and let me do my job. I can't have civilians in the middle of a crime scene or a potential standoff.''

Penny raised her brow. "How many sets of handcuffs do you have, Chief?" She reached in the squad car and retrieved the police-issued shotgun from its rack.

Joe's scowl had Nathan backing up a step. Penny didn't budge.

When the door of the house opened, four weapons were raised and cocked in unison, four voices harmonizing. "Freeze."

"Do what they say, Gramps!" Nathan called, fear ringing in his voice. Clearly, crime wasn't an arena he was comfortable in—or else he was one heck of an actor.

The old man in the doorway tossed a gun into the yard and held up his hands. In one of them was a piece of paper. "She stole…the witch—"

His shoulders slumped in defeat as he came out of the doorway and down the steps. "She stole my…"

At the bottom step, he collapsed.

Penny rushed forward despite Joe's admonishment to wait. Nathan joined them beside Al Lantrelle's body.

She checked for a pulse, then looked up at the still handcuffed Nathan. Whether he was an accomplice or not, the man was still his kin.

Nathan nodded. "It was only a matter of days. I think the only thing that's kept him going, that even gave him strength to assault you in the first place, was knowing that the gold was still here."

Joe took the note out of the old man's hand. "I guess it wasn't here after all."

"What?" Penny and Nathan said in unison. She took the paper from him and read it. The note was from Agnes to Al.

Dear Al,

   Looking for something you left behind? But we both know it couldn't be me. I was never your cup of tea, was I? Well, I've beaten you at your own game, you old goat, betrayed you just as you betrayed me, not once, but twice.

   I found your gold bars, turned them in, and it gives me the greatest pleasure to report that I've lived and invested nicely on the reward money they brought. I hope you've dreamed often of the riches you'll never see.

   And I hope you rot in hell.

                                        Agnes

If there wasn't a corpse lying at her feet, Penny might have laughed at the irony of the whole episode. Who would have thought her grandmother would have possessed such a sense of drama?

Penny stood and looked at Nathan. "Who wrote those letters you showed me?"

"I did. I didn't know how else to get to know you. Gramps really did leave your grandmother at the altar all those years ago. Then twenty years back he stole the gold and needed a place to hide out for a bit until the heat died down. He came back to Darby on the guise of looking up an old flame and apologizing. That's how I got the idea for the letters.''

"He needed a place to stash his loot and he toyed with Agnes's affections once more for his own gain," Georgia said, happy to get into the story.

Penny had an urge to slug the lout, but didn't think it would look good to hit a dead man. She nearly slugged the grandson, a sort of blow by proxy.

But Joe came up behind her, eased an arm around her waist, pulled her back to him, lending his strength and his support, and keeping her from damaging any more body parts.

Two more squad cars pulled up at the curb, officers getting out with guns drawn. A white sedan stopped a few paces back. The mayor.

"Looks like we're fixing to have a town meeting in my side yard."

Joe gave her waist a squeeze. "You going to be okay?"

She was trembling and knew he could feel it. Adrenaline was ebbing and her throat and lungs burned. She'd nearly been killed and a man had died at her feet.

She nodded. "You ought to be worrying about yourself. The mayor will expect an accounting from you. Worry over the safety of the streets and your future children."

"Our children will be fine."

He said it so easily. So confidently. Her heart felt like brittle china.

"I gotta tell you, Penny. You've certainly livened up the town," Mayor Upton said, giving Georgia and

Wanetta a wide berth since they both still held shot-guns in their hands.

"I didn't mean to."

"You can't help it. It's who you are as much as anything going on around you."

But she wasn't who these people thought she was. And she definitely wasn't who Joe thought she was. He was looking at her as though she were the future mother of his children.

He had no idea how far from reality that was.

No matter how much she ached for things to be different, they weren't. Her future had been determined a night many years ago, in a dingy motel room.

Take your pills. Take your pills. Take your pills.

Penny closed her eyes against the memory of her beautiful mother, so childlike, so disturbed.

Her mother...the reason Penny would take her own pills every day to prevent the repeat of a troubled life.

Joe turned her in his arms, tipped up her chin. His gaze was intense. He saw so much. And she knew what he saw in her face.

"Go do your job, Chief."

His jaw clenched. "To hell with the job. Don't do this, Penny."

She shook her head. "We'll talk later."

He hesitated. She knew he wanted to pin her down, demand that she tell him what was going on in her mind, give him the chance to argue the barriers she'd set against love and family and all the things she wanted.

But duty intruded.

"You call the coroner and handle the arrest," she suggested. "I'll deal with crowd control."

It was time to go. The mystery was solved. She'd stayed longer than she should have, given them both false hope.

She'd taken a few weeks for herself. But what had she accomplished?

She'd be leaving two hearts in Darby—both of them broken. Joe's and her own.

Chapter Fourteen

Penny hadn't let Joe stay the night. With the crisis past, she needed time to gather her strength for what she knew was to come.

Their parting.

She spent most of the night cleaning up the mess made by Al Lantrelle, nailing back the floorboards in the back bedroom where the gold had once been hidden.

And now, she had a few more loose ends to tie up. She glanced at her contact lens case, then put it away in her makeup bag.

She'd come back to town with visions of taking Darby by storm, of breezing in and out, presenting herself as a glamorous, mysterious, intriguing package. And she'd succeeded.

But that wasn't who she was.

She would leave today—tomorrow at the latest. As soon as she had the details all compartmentalized. But she would leave as who she really was.

Plain Penny Archer. No more masquerade.

She showered and deliberately put on her wire-rimmed glasses, leaving her face scrubbed free of makeup, then twisted her hair up in a clip. A couple of strands fell forward to brush her jawbone.

As though putting on a uniform, she donned tailored slacks, a button-down blouse, summer blazer and glove-soft penny loafers.

The woman staring back at her in the mirror should have looked familiar. Instead, she looked foreign. Efficient, but sad. And even though she wore her traditional satin and lace beneath the no-nonsense look, it just didn't feel the same.

"Oh, get over it, Penny."

She started to call for the collie, then remembered he was over at Georgia and Wanetta's. The aunts had fallen in love with the little dog and the feeling was evidently mutual.

One loose end tied up.

She grabbed her keys and let herself out the door, cringing at the crunched trunk of the Cadillac. Though it ran fine, it looked like it had been in a demolition derby.

The town was gearing up for the Fourth of July parade that would take place three days from now. Barricades were already in place on the sidewalks, ready to block off the streets along the parade route. She could hear the high school's marching band practicing over in the football field a few blocks away, the brassy music and beat of drums and cymbals bringing back memories of hot summer sun and concession stands, of people lining the sidewalks and spilling out onto front lawns to watch the celebration.

Of children shrieking in glee and babies bawling and parents simply enjoying family and community.

Oh, she wanted that image—that reality—so bad she nearly doubled over.

Pulling up in front of the bank, she went next door to Russ Reilly's law office.

His receptionist, Mary Anne Hudson, had graduated from school with Penny. They hadn't run in the same circles, and Penny couldn't remember ever actually speaking with the woman, but Mary Anne hopped right out of her chair and came around the desk offering a hug as though they'd been best pals.

"Penny. It's so wonderful to see you again after all these years."

Penny smiled, for some reason feeling a bit self-conscious in her tailored clothes. It was much easier to hide behind a tough-girl image rather than the no-nonsense one.

She reminded herself the masquerade was over.

"Good to see you, too. Is Russ in?"

"Hey, Penny," Russ said from the doorway of his office. "Come on in."

She went into his small office. Tastefully furnished in muted grays and dark oak, it was a comfortable space. A far cry from high-dollar corporate law, but Russ seemed at home.

"Have a seat."

"Actually, I just stopped by to pick up my grandmother's safe deposit key."

He opened a file and took out an envelope. "I heard about the commotion at your place last night."

Penny laughed. "Word certainly travels fast. As always." She colored when she realized what she'd said. In high school, word of Joe's bet had traveled fast. And Russ had been one of the circle of guys who'd been in on it.

He handed her the envelope, obviously not thinking about the same incident as she was. "You're quite newsworthy. Half the people in town are envious of you and the other half want to *be* you."

She rolled her eyes. "Get out."

He shrugged and grinned. "I've got to count myself in that group, too. There're a lot of us who would have liked to take down Don Gilard."

Penny felt a tug of disgust at the thought of Gilard, and a sense of satisfaction that she'd gotten in the last lick. "Believe me, I enjoyed that immensely."

His grin widened. "So my wife told me."

The reminder made her really look at Russ. He'd been a popular jock in school, just like Joe. And Pam had been just one of the girls who hadn't stood out. She'd been funny and fun, but not necessarily popular.

"Are you happy here?" she asked, then wanted to take back the question. It wasn't like her to pry, or to get personal.

"Very. Pam's the best thing that's ever happened to me. She keeps me laughing. I never know what to expect. I'm glad I settled on family life in Darby."

"It suits you." She fidgeted with the envelope. "Well, I guess I better get on over to the bank. I never even thought to check this box. Grandmother didn't exactly live like she had money."

Russ shook his head, an agreement. "She never said a word to me, and I was her attorney. She refused to define her assets in her will, told me to just write it up that the entire estate was to pass to you.''

Penny nodded, wondering if she really deserved her grandmother's estate since she hadn't been back here in twelve years.

"So, will you be staying?" Russ asked, jolting her.

"No."

His brows rose. "But I thought…" His words trailed off. "None of my business, I guess."

Penny started to flick her hair behind her ear, then remembered she'd twisted it up. She held out her hand to Russ. "It was nice seeing you. Thank you for taking care of my grandmother's things."

"Just doing my job." He hesitated. "Ah, hell. Are you sure you won't reconsider staying? Pam's going to be disappointed. And a lot of other people, too."

Joe.

Penny pressed a smile on her lips. "It's just not in the cards, Russ. I'll stop by and see Pam and the kids before I leave."

"Thanks. My sons will be crushed, though. They think you're the best thing since video games."

Penny remembered little Steven, wanting so badly to hang out with the older children, his tiny face scrunched up in concentration as she'd steadied the air rifle at his shoulder, helped him win an ugly purple dragon.

Damn it, there were too many great kids and families in this town.

She had to get out of here. She was going to lose it.

"Tomorrow there'll be a new game on the market and they'll forget all about me. Take care, Russ."

She left the office and went next door to the bank to remove the contents of her grandmother's safe deposit box. She felt a little like a bank robber when she put her hands around the bundled stacks of cash. About twenty thousand. And an absolute fortune in stock and bond certificates.

How had Agnes kept this size portfolio private?

Leaving the bank, Penny noticed Lanie Dubois eyeing her, and some devil came over her. Unable to resist, she placed her hand on her purse, toyed with the zipper.

Lanie's eyes widened and she suddenly became engrossed in the paperwork in front of her on her desk.

Laughing, Penny let herself out the door and headed toward Kelly's bookstore.

Hot summer sun beat on the pavement, softening the tar in the streets. Heat waves rose off the hoods of the cars angled at the curb.

Inside the bookstore, the air-conditioning flowed at a comfortable temperature.

"Hey, Kel," she called, noticing her friend sitting on the floor, perusing a children's book.

"Penny!" Kelly hopped up and put the book back on the shelf. "I was just checking out the merchandise. We're going to have children's storytelling hour after the parade."

"Sounds like fun. I remember when we used to go to that over at the library."

"And usually got in trouble for being loud and rambunctious."

"You were a terrible influence on me," Penny said with a smile.

"So what brings you out in the heat in your secret agent clothes? You look great, by the way. Are you giving your account of what went on at your place last night?"

"No. Joe was there and I gave my statement at the scene." She looked great?

"Isn't it wild about that old beau of your grandmother's showing up like that? And stashing loot in her house?"

"I'm providing plenty of fodder for the book Pam's going to write."

Kelly smoothed her hands down the front of her summer dress and nodded to a couple of chairs set up along the far wall for readers. "Come on. Business is slow. We'll sit and you'll tell me what's on your mind."

"Nothing earth shaking," Penny said, but sat in one of the armed chairs anyway. "I just wanted to stop by and let you know I'll be leaving."

Kelly was silent for a long moment. "I would have bet money you'd be staying."

"I can't."

"Now we're getting somewhere."

"What do you mean?"

"Can't. That's a word that shouts. Why can't you?"

"I have a job I love."

"But you love Joe more. And you'd give up that job in a minute but something's stopping you. I want to know what it is."

Penny reached beneath her glasses and rubbed her eyes. She'd never been a transparent sort of person. Joe was the open book. Penny was the one with all the secrets. So why did everyone suddenly seem to see right through her? Were her feelings so obvious?

"Joe wants a family, Kelly."

"So?"

"So, you know what my mother was."

Kelly frowned. "What does your mother have to do with you and Joe?"

"She was sick. I could carry that gene and pass it on to a child."

Kelly threw her hands up. "Well, so could I! Get a life for heaven's sake."

Penny was so astonished by Kelly's outburst she was speechless for several seconds, long enough for Kelly to gather her composure and her breath.

"I never told you, but I'm adopted."

"You're...but your parents...your family's so great, so close."

"Of course. They love me. Blood doesn't make a family. My point is, I have no idea where or who I came from. I've never even thought about finding out. And that means I have no earthly idea what's in my gene pool. But that didn't stop me from having my own family. I've got three beautiful, healthy, happy kids."

Penny still couldn't get over the bombshell her friend had dropped.

"Pen, genetics only forms one part of a person's makeup. We have plenty of control over how we act and react. None of us are without flaws. Lord knows

I've got a ton of them, and so do you. But look at you." She waved a hand over Penny. "Your record's pretty darn good so far."

Penny bit her bottom lip. "I've been an idiot."

"So what's new?"

A smile grew. "I can always trust you to keep my feet on the ground."

"Hey, what are friends for if not to insult you once in a while." Her voice softened. "Have you talked to Joe about this?"

She shook her head.

"Don't you think he deserves to make his own decision?"

Penny swallowed hard. "That's what I'm so afraid of. It's a lot easier to leave with my own belief system intact. I don't know if I can stand it if he rejects me."

"Penny—"

"Not everyone is like you Kelly. Joe might feel differently."

"Do you love him?"

"More than anything."

"Then I think you have to give him the choice."

ALL THE WAY HOME, Penny's palms were slick against the steering wheel, no matter how low she turned the air-conditioning thermostat. Her heart was alternately filled with hope and despair. She'd had hopes before and seen them dashed. She wasn't used to taking something for herself.

Joe was leaning against his truck when she pulled up in the Cadillac, his arms folded across his chest.

Boots encased his feet and the sand-colored Stetson rode his head.

He looked like a man on a mission. Well over six feet of stubborn attitude and determination.

Like a man prepared to get his way and willing to lay siege if need be.

Penny felt a host of butterflies take wing in her stomach. Dear Lord, she loved this man.

Her heart vaulted into her throat as he straightened away from the truck and came toward her, his gaze leaving her for only a second to glance at the smashed trunk of her car.

He stopped in front of her, his hands fisted at his sides as though he wanted to reach for her but was afraid.

His eyes traveled over her body, lingering like the sweetest caress. The visual journey seemed to take forever, and it was all Penny could do to stand still, to not shrink back into her shell.

"Wow."

Her heart sank, but she put on a sassy smile anyway. "Just me. Plain Penny."

His eyes lifted to hers, astonished. "Plain? Baby, you couldn't be plain if you tried."

Well, she *was* trying. Was her mirror showing a different image than everyone else was seeing?

He reached out, grazed her cheek with his fingertips, brushed back a curly strand of hair that had escaped her twist, then gestured at her body with his hand as though words escaped him.

"This is the woman who can make a suspect quake in his shoes. Innate sensuality, simple elegance.

Makes me want to peel you right out of those sensible clothes. I came here to yell at you.''

That made her smile. Compliments to threats without so much as a breath to separate them. ''Want to go inside?''

''Might be best. I've got a few things to say and as much as I know the aunts would enjoy the entertainment, I'm not up for it.''

She nearly asked him what he *was* up for, but decided she was feeling too fragile right now to be at her best.

Once inside, Penny suffered an attack of nerves. She paced, wondered how to broach the subject.

Joe did it for her. ''I want to know why you're pulling away from me. Why you're leaving.''

''How did you…?'' Russ, she thought. Or Kelly. Did it matter? In Darby, folks would always find out news faster than God Himself. ''I'm…you want children.''

''Yes.''

She stared at him, pleaded with her eyes for him to understand. ''I told you about my mother…I'm afraid to have children,'' she said in a rush. ''I don't want to pass on a flaw.''

''Pass on—'' He put his hands on his hips, glared at her from beneath the brim of his hat. ''Is that what this is all about?''

She shrugged and nodded.

''For Pete's sake, Penny. My great-grandfather was as crazy as a loon and my uncle drank himself to death. Life is a gamble. But it's short and we have to make every moment count. Today. With hope and love." He gripped her arms, pulled her to him. "For me, that hope is you."

Her throat ached. "I keep seeing my mother's face," she whispered into his shirtfront. "She looked so normal, so peaceful lying there on that ratty bedspread, the empty bottle of pills in her hand."

He held her tight. "That's something no child should have witnessed."

"It shaped me. Made me think I was flawed."

"Then I'm just as flawed. If we live with what-ifs we might as well give up. The thing is, I don't need a family to complete me. But I do need you, Penny. I love you. Not as a potential mother to my children, but as my mate. I need *you*. Not the children you can or can't give me. Marry me."

"Joe—"

"I'm the man who loves you best, Pen. I always have and I always will. I can't let you go again. Please don't ask me to—"

"Yes."

"—You have my heart. I'll spend my last breath convincing you of that, reminding you, letting you know that you can trust me with yours—" He stopped abruptly, looked at her. "What did you say?"

"I said yes."

"Oh, thank God." His mouth crushed down on hers. It was a kiss filled with so much love Penny thought she'd surely melt right at his feet.

When they both needed air he lifted his mouth and kissed her brow, her cheek, pushed her glasses to the top of her head and kissed her eyelids.

"You really are going to have to tell me what kind

of an agent you are. I need to know if you'll be going off on clandestine assignments, or if I'll need to turn over the running of the ranch to someone else so I can relocate to where you need to be.''

"You'd be willing to leave Darby for me?"

"Absolutely."

Her heart was near to bursting. "I'm not actually a Texas Confidential agent—yet. I'm Mitchell's assistant, and though I know every case and pretty much run the joint, I don't do assignments.''

"Do they know what a talent they're wasting?"

She smiled and kissed him. It was the most perfect thing he could have said. "Before I came home, I'd accepted a position to become an agent. My training was supposed to start the middle of July.''

"Was?"

"Was. I love you, Joe. You're all the adventure I need.''

"Frankly, I could use a little less adventure. And I'm probably going to kick myself for suggesting this, but have you considered applying for chief of police here in Darby? I have it on the best authority that there's about to be an opening. The current chief wants to be a full-time cowboy.''

"Mmm, and he'll be a very sexy one." She gave the brim of his hat a tug, thinking she'd urge his lips back to hers.

He chuckled. "Pay attention, woman. I'm trying to plan your future.''

"Do carry on. I'm intrigued."

"I figured you would be. It's a good plan, Pen. You're more than qualified. The mayor's totally impressed by you and everybody already believes you're a 007 Bond person. The town'll stay in line just in fear of you pulling some watch weapon or something and zapping cars to make them explode.''

She laughed. ''Enough. Yes. Yes. Yes. To the job, to the marriage...to love.'' She sobered, placed her palm along the side of his handsome face. ''I do love you, Joe. You're the only man I've ever loved.''

''Man alive, Penny. You humble me.''

She kissed him again. ''I'll need a good department backing me up.''

''Darren and Larry are the best.''

''Good. Because I *will* want babies with you.''

Joe felt his heart soften and click. Then a thought had him sweating. Perhaps he hadn't thought this all the way through. The vivid image of her car barreling out of the garage, the knowledge of how close she'd come to death, the sight of blood on her head, lying unconscious on the porch.

''Now that I think about it, I'm not sure I'm so keen on my pregnant wife drawing her gun on bad guys and ramming cars out of garages and getting in highway pursuits. Maybe you ought to just come out to the ranch and try your hand at being a cowgirl.''

Penny laughed. ''You're just afraid I'll show you up to the town because I'm a better shot and a whiz on the computer.''

He growled deep in his throat and lifted her in his arms. ''Let's just see who shows who up.'' Joe knew they'd always be one-upping each other. He loved it. And he loved her.

"Don't get too cocky, cowboy. Makes the landing a lot harder when you lose."

"Oh, I'll never lose." He pressed his mouth to hers, so tenderly, so reverently, so filled with love. His voice was soft and filled with promise. "I got the girl."

Epilogue

Through the mahogany church doors, Penny could see wood pews filled to capacity. Darby's citizens were casting furtive glances at the Texas Confidential agents and their wives, fairly buzzing with excitement as though they were in the midst of celebrities. Gorgeous men, they truly could have been celebrities.

Penny felt tears back up in her throat. This was her family all around her. Brady Morgan and his wife Grace—Catherine now, she remembered, due to the witness protection program and her marriage to Brady. Jake Cantrell, his wife Abby and their six-year-old daughter, Elena. Rafe and Kendra Alvarez, both glowing with the news of Kendra's pregnancy—twins! Cody Gannon and his wife, Sarah, cradling their seven-month-old baby girl, Joy. All had gone through near tragedies to come together, making their unions so much more special.

Behind them was Slim Dillon, the Smoking Barrel's craggy old ranch hand looking spiffed up in a western shirt and bolo tie, and Rosa Chavez, for once without her apron. And Maddie, the woman who'd been in love with Mitchell for years and he'd only recently had the good sense to recognize it and marry her.

"Ready?" Mitchell asked.

She looked up into the handsome face of the man who'd been a second father to her. The ex-Texas Ranger had a hand in the pocket of his tuxedo pants, no doubt worrying the silver lighter he always kept close.

"I'm a nervous wreck."

"You're beautiful." Her dress was ivory antique satin, an old-fashioned gown with an attached train that spread out a yard behind her. Wanetta had brought it home from her boutique and taken care of the alterations herself. The rest of the town had scurried into action, putting together an elaborate show as though they hosted weddings every day.

"And you'll be fine," Mitchell continued. "You always were the smartest and strongest of us all."

"No—"

"Yes," he said softly, gruffly. "We're going to miss you, Penny. You've been an invaluable colleague all these years, but more than that, you've been the daughter I never had."

Penny swallowed hard, whispered the words he couldn't say. "I love you, too."

The organist segued into the traditional wedding

march song, and Penny's hand gripped the crook of Mitchell's arm.

All eyes turned to her.

As one, it seemed, the entire congregation stood and began to applaud. Penny had never seen anything like it—applause usually took place *after* the ceremony. Tears of joy were shed, murmurs of awe.

The lilies in her hands shook as she lifted her gaze to Joe's. Handsome and tall, he stepped forward from his place in front by the altar as though he intended to come down the aisle and escort her himself.

But he didn't need to come for her because Mitchell finally urged her forward, his limp barely noticeable as he proudly covered her hand that gripped so tightly on his arm.

When they stopped in front of Joe, Penny wondered if she would be able to stand without Mitchell's aid.

The utter, profound look of love on Joe's face gave her courage. With his eyes alone, he made her feel radiant.

"Who gives this woman in marriage?" the reverend asked.

Five male voices chorused, "We do!"

Penny turned around and frowned. Brady, Jake, Rafe and Cody were standing, grins splitting their faces.

"Honestly," she muttered, yet felt her heart nearly burst with love. All that testosterone under one roof had annoyed her at times while she'd worked with them, yet she'd secretly cherished these men. They were family. And they were giving her away with love...for love.

She turned back to Joe, smiled into his loving hazel eyes. "Guess this means we've got their vote of approval."

He cupped her cheek, tenderly, reverently, making every woman—and quite a few of the men—in the congregation sigh.

"I don't need anybody's approval. You are smart and strong and sexy and gorgeous and fun and interesting...you're the woman I love. And for that, I'll never need approval. You're my best girl, Pen."

Although they were rushing the ceremony, Joe leaned down and kissed his bride. No one objected or stopped to point out it wasn't time yet.

When he raised his head and gazed into her eyes, fireworks burst outside. Bottle rockets and roman candles left over from the Fourth of July parade whistled and boomed above the church.

Joe grinned. "I think we've delayed a little too long. It's time for the fireworks and we haven't yet said I do. What do you say, Chief?"

Hearing him call *her* chief brought a bubble of laughter. But softer emotions overrode mirth.

"I do, Joe," she said softly. "For every day and every breath, forever, I do."

The reverend cleared his throat. "Is it my turn now?"

Mitchell Forbes—seconded by the rest of the Texas Confidential agents—assured him that it was.

* * * * *

We hope you've enjoyed Penny's story!
If you've missed any of the books in
Harlequin Intrigue's Texas Confidential *series,*
you can still order them from
Customer Service.
HI 581—*THE BODYGUARD'S ASSIGNMENT*
by Amanda Stevens

HI 585—*THE AGENT'S SECRET CHILD*
by B.J. Daniels

HI 589—*THE SPECIALIST*
by Dani Sinclair

HI 593—*THE OUTSIDER'S REDEMPTION*
by Joanna Wayne

And beginning in August 2001, look for
MONTANA CONFIDENTIAL.
Four brand-new adventures brought to you
by Harlequin Intrigue.

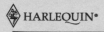

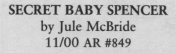

Tyler Brides

It happened one weekend...

Quinn and Molly Spencer are delighted to accept three
bookings for their newly opened B&B, Breakfast Inn Bed,
located in America's favorite hometown, Tyler, Wisconsin.

But Gina Santori is anything but thrilled to discover her
best friend has tricked her into sharing a room with
the man who broke her heart eight years ago....

And Delia Mayhew can hardly believe that she's
gotten herself locked in the Breakfast Inn Bed
basement with the sexiest man in America.

Then there's Rebecca Salter. She's turned up at the
Inn in her wedding gown. Minus her groom.

*Come home to Tyler for three delightful novellas
by three of your favorite authors: Kristine Rolofson,
Heather MacAllister and Jacqueline Diamond.*

HARLEQUIN®
Makes any time special ™

Visit us at www.eHarlequin.com

PHTB

From bestselling
Harlequin American Romance author

CATHY GILLEN THACKER

comes

TEXAS VOWS

A McCABE FAMILY SAGA

Sam McCabe had vowed to always
do right by his five boys—but after
the loss of his wife, he needed the small-town security
of his hometown, Laramie, Texas, to live up to that
commitment. Except, coming home would bring him
back to a woman he'd sworn to stay away from.
It will be one vow that Sam can't keep....

On sale March 2001

Available at your favorite retail outlet.

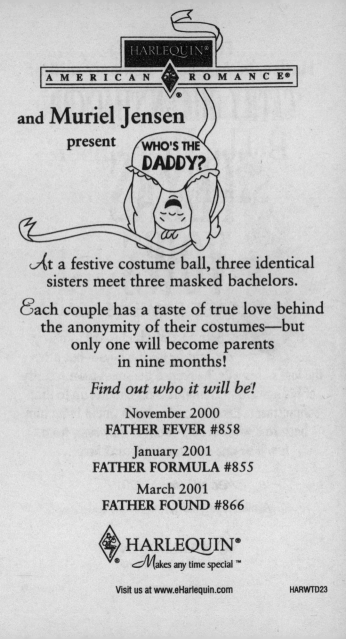

HARLEQUIN®

AMERICAN ◆ ROMANCE®

and **Muriel Jensen**

present

WHO'S THE
DADDY?

*A*t a festive costume ball, three identical
sisters meet three masked bachelors.

*E*ach couple has a taste of true love behind
the anonymity of their costumes—but
only one will become parents
in nine months!

Find out who it will be!

November 2000
FATHER FEVER #858

January 2001
FATHER FORMULA #855

March 2001
FATHER FOUND #866

HARLEQUIN®
*M*akes any time special ™

CELEBRATE VALENTINE'S DAY WITH HARLEQUIN®'S LATEST TITLE—

Stolen Memories

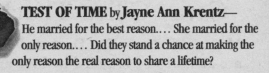

Available in trade-size format, this collector's edition contains three full-length novels by *New York Times* bestselling authors Jayne Ann Krentz and Tess Gerritsen, along with national bestselling author Stella Cameron.

TEST OF TIME by **Jayne Ann Krentz**—

He married for the best reason.... She married for the only reason.... Did they stand a chance at making the only reason the real reason to share a lifetime?

THIEF OF HEARTS by **Tess Gerritsen**—

Their distrust of each other was only as strong as their desire. And Jordan began to fear that Diana was more than just a thief of hearts.

MOONTIDE by **Stella Cameron**—

For Andrew, Greer's return is a miracle. It had broken his heart to let her go. Now fate has brought them back together. And he won't lose her again...

Make this Valentine's Day one to remember!

Look for this exciting collector's edition on sale January 2001 at your favorite retail outlet.

HARLEQUIN®
Makes any time special ™

Visit us at www.eHarlequin.com   PHSM